OUT *of the* FRYING PAN, STRAIGHT *into the* FIRE

OUT *of the* FRYING PAN, STRAIGHT *into the* FIRE

TINA CLINGER

iUniverse, Inc.
Bloomington

Out of the Frying Pan, Straight into the Fire

This is a work of fiction. All of the characters, names, incidents, organizations, and dialogue in this novel are either the products of the author's imagination or are used fictitiously.

iUniverse books may be ordered through booksellers or by contacting:

iUniverse
1663 Liberty Drive
Bloomington, IN 47403
www.iuniverse.com
1-800-Authors (1-800-288-4677)

Because of the dynamic nature of the Internet, any web addresses or links contained in this book may have changed since publication and may no longer be valid. The views expressed in this work are solely those of the author and do not necessarily reflect the views of the publisher, and the publisher hereby disclaims any responsibility for them.

Any people depicted in stock imagery provided by Thinkstock are models, and such images are being used for illustrative purposes only.
Certain stock imagery © Thinkstock.

ISBN: 978-1-4759-0993-7 (sc)
ISBN: 978-1-4759-0994-4 (ebk)

Printed in the United States of America

iUniverse rev. date: 04/14/2012

Contents

First, I would like to dedicate and thank my husband Dennis Clinger; my three sons Tachmonite, Frank III, and Charles Shammah Butler; my four brothers Christopher Sr., Jouron (an extra special thanks Grampy for your assurance and financial support), Reuben and Edward Kees; my parents Tyrone and Edwena Kees; my sister Tara and nephew Jonathan for all of their encouragement, support, patience, lending of their ears/eyes and just plain belief that I could accomplish putting my love for writing on paper!

Secondly, I want to thank my co-workers past and present Araceli (Chely)Gutierrez, Sherrita James, Shera Bush, Shaneka Sears, Nikki Hamilton, Roger Benge and Tasha Wright for letting me chatter on and on about my book and not stapling my lips together. Katorry Tyler (author of "Forgive or Forget"), my mentor/co-worker you hold a dear place in my heart because you inspired me to stop talking about it and get it done!

Thirdly, to Drew Brees, Sean Peyton and the New Orleans Saints for winning the Superbowl XLIV that help me believe that if you work hard you can achieve it. The editors, consultants and staff of Iuniverse Publishing Co and Jackie Alston for whom brought the passion out of me with lessons 1 and 2 lol!

Finally and most importantly to my all mighty God, whom has guided me through life's path and even when I stumble he picks me up, gently places a hand in my back, forgive me of my transgressions and continue to stir me on life's gracious journey.

Tina Clinger works as a Senior Associate with a local bank in Arkansas. She enjoys writing and have many tall tales locked in her mind safe to be picked. Previously Mrs. Clinger has only written entertaining articles online. She has three sons, three grandchildren and lives with her husband in Little Rock.

The Beginning

O h boy, it's the first warm Saturday here in Ponde, Louisiana and instead of drinking a nice cold watermelon wine cooler and sitting back enjoying a piece of chicken that she saw barbecuing on the grill as she passed through the backyard into the house, Kya found herself running for cover as shots ranged out. Just as she crouched in corner she was wishing she hadn't sat her purse down, with her cell phone, on the patio table. As she peeked over the sofa to see who and where the gunshots were coming from she spotted Bruce. He seemed to be reloading his gun and mumbling something to himself as he stomped around throwing things and just plain wreaking havoc on what was once a beautiful home.

Guess your wonder whose Bruce and why Kya is hiding from him? Bruce is Kya's home girl Chandenise husband. She invited Kya to her new two story, five bedroom, four bathroom home for a barbeque but judging from the knocked over broken furniture and bullet holes in the walls it appears Kya walked into a war. Kya wondered where her best friend was as she surveyed the room once more from her temporary safe haven, she spotted Chandenise on the floor. She was just lying there motionless with blood gushing from her neck. "Oh my God Chandenise" Kya gasped in disbelief as she slid from one end of the sofa to the other to get a closer look at her friend's body. Since Bruce had taken his tirade to one of the other rooms in the house, Kya was able to crawl over to Chandenise body and through her tears she could see that her friend throat was cut from ear to ear.

Kya crouched to the patio and managed to get her cell phone from her purse before Bruce made his way back into the living-room. Dialing 911 and shaking like a leaf she whispery relayed the scene to the 911 operator as she took refuge behind the plush sectional sofa again. She had no idea what happen to drive this man whom every time she saw him he was calm, cool and collected to behave in such a disastrous way. Bruce had a deranged look on his face as he walked pass the sofa and headed toward the back yard and Kya made a mad dash for the stairs to check for other injured bodies. She was hoping that Chandenise's mom and daughter wasn't home and had become victims too.

As Kya quickly and quietly on shaky legs searched through the bedrooms she could hear gunshots in the distance letting her know Bruce hadn't made it back to the house yet. So she made her way back down the stairs to the kitchen and that's when she spotted a guy crawling out of the rose colored bottom cabinets. She grabbed the nearby broom and began to beat the guy upside the head, while screaming I got him! I got him! As the guy and Kya tussled about he said "Ms. Martinley I didn't do it, it was Bruce! It was Bruce"! As Kya took in his words she noticed the guy was sporting a bullet wound to the thigh.

The unknown man told Kya that Bruce came home and went insane when he saw the two of them talking. He said Bruce shouted "I knew it you slutty bitch, it's true you can't turn a whore into a housewife". Mrs. England tried to explain to him that nothing was going on and uttered that even if there were she could do whatever she wanted because they were legally separated. Mrs. England also told him to leave and ushered him toward the front door when Bruce suddenly stopped turned slit her throat, dropped the knife, pulled out his gun and that's when I took off running; getting hit in the leg.

With the wailing of police siren in the air, Bruce made it back into the house, followed the commotion to the kitchen and aimed his gun straight in the direction of the stranger. Once he spotted Kya he just started screaming "I warned her Kya, she made me do it. I told her once we got married and she cheat on me I was going to kill her! Now I must kill him too!" Bruce aimed the gun at the stranger and pulled the trigger as the guy went down Kya tried to catch him but manage to fall hitting her head on the rose and mauve marble countertop instead. As she laid there in her somewhat out of body state Kya began to recall the day they formed the now defunct teenage club B*A*C*K and how each of the members lives had unfolded over the years.

Chandenise and I have been friends since the first day at Ponde Senior High. Because we hung in different circles I knew her vaguely from around middle school and because my family had moved two blocks down and three blocks over (right next to the Tyler home) from our previous home my school district had changed. So going to Bell High home of the Wolves was out for me. Mom dropped me off at the front entrance and I remembered staring at this big yellow otter holding a blue club painted on the front door. How good can their sports teams be with a mascot called, Oscar the Otter.

Walking and fixated on the golden mammal painted on the walls I bumped into Chandenise. She introduced herself as Chandenise Tyler the finest women on the face of the earth with a butt any man would love to touch. I said my name was Kya Martinley and I do believe were neighbors. Chandenise simply say yes we are then whispered stick with me and I can make these years wonderfully fun for you.

Now an intro like that means this girl was high on herself and since Kya was intent on making this new school a good change for her, a new friend yet familiar face would be nice. As the bell rang Chandenise suggested for Kya meet her at the tree to the right of the cafeteria exit for lunch turned and sashayed up the stairs. Kya proceed down the wide hallway, where all of the opened doors looked like mouths open with its tongue hanging out to the office to get her schedule, then off to homeroom.

As luck would have it, Chandenise and Kya were in the same fourth period science class and as soon as she saw her she waved her multicolored nails for Kya to come over. Chandenise was sitting in the second row, second seat and to the left of her was a red skin, red head sister and they were chatting away about some boy named Terrion that apparently was the hottest thing since the cell phone. Kya later learned that the sister name was Airis and she and Chandenise were cousins. They sat through class passing notes with no one paying any attention to what Mrs. Branks, their teacher, were saying. The bell rang for lunch and from there the next three years seem to zoom by.

Chandenise was popular, into sport, loved the fellas and by her own admission had an occasional problem with the young men and was the subject of gossip by the young ladies. It didn't matter though because the guys of Ponde High were smitten with Chandenise and her little protégés. By their senior year Kya's body had finally caught up with her age, therefore like Chandenise she turning quite a few heads herself as they strolled down the halls of Ponde High.

One particular morning, while in the girl's bathroom the pair came across a young lady bawling her eyes out. Chandenise, being her usual selfish self-ignored the situation but Kya couldn't stand to see a person upset like that. So she walked over to quivering lady and asked her what's wrong? This young lady told a tale of how she tried to please her boyfriend by having a threesome and that morning he called and broke up with her. She said her name was Bailey Denfard and they had been dating since they were juniors and she thought they were going to be married.

This sparked the words of wisdom from the almighty Chandenise; "Girl quit your blubbering over these young men. Hell this is your time to use them and throw them away; they don't know what they want except our triangle trove and hell I make them pay for it. Shit, I guarantee he was seeing others while he was with you anyway. What you need to do now is show him what he is missing out on". From then on Chandenise and Kya had formed a friendship with Bailey and along with cousin Airis, formed a club.

Kya remember the day it happen. They were all over at Bailey's house and Airis had just been dumped by her boyfriend, which sent her into one of her verbal pacing rampage. It's funny, Airis is the somewhat quite one but when she is angry all of her 180 lbs, 5'7" comes roaring out turning her already light red skin into a shade of crimson that matched her hair which seem to make the freckles across her nose stand out even more. Chandenise leaped off the bed and stopped Airis in her tracks by turning her to the mirror and said it's his lost look at you you're a vision of red perfection with a butt almost as roundly perfect like mines. Bailey jumped up and she too was staring into the door length mirror that hung in her closet admiring her butt. This is when Chandenise said lets form a club.

What type of club Kya asked? Chandenise replied you know a club for sisters with big butts. Namely us four of course! Kya looked around scanning the company she was with. There was Chandenise, with her man using don't care about nobody but me attitude yet had a surprising gentle creed with her mother, she stood 5'5" 150 lbs, oval shape face, hazel contact eyes, caramel skin, shoulder length coal black hair that seem to flow to the music of the wind every time she took a step with a funny zigzag scar on her left check just below the ear; Bailey, the miss go-getter but I will do anything to fit girl was a golden caramel skin 5'5", 140 lbs, dimples, big wide eyes and dark brown hair that was always in a lopsided ponytail whom always appears to be hiding something; Airis the quiet angry lady and herself—the peace maker, dark chocolate standing at 5'3" 150 lbs soaking wet, slightly squinted eyes, craters for dimples, shoulder length uneven black hair and bowlegs. However, there were two things they all shared, big butts and guy problems.

Just like that they formed a club using the acronym BACK with their motto being do it to them before they do it to us. They set up rules and dues, went down to the local mall and had their pictures taken, ordered pretty multicolored shirts with their club name, and vowed to send the young men and men of Ponde, Louisiana a message. Chandenise nominated herself president and she meant business, the business of using and revenge that lasted even through college.

Bailey Dabbles

As she was driving up to the club Four-Leaf Clover, Bailey kept thinking about the crazy thing she was about to do. So she put the car in reverse and drove around the block two times. Her heart wanted to just go in and act like it's no big deal but her head kept telling her to go home, beside you have no idea what your was doing she said out loud to herself.

After a few more trips around she pulled the car into the parking space far away but behind the bar next to a tie dye colored dumpster. Bailey sat there not realizing she was holding her breath, until the phone rang. It was Mindy, a girl she met on the Rainbow One Night Stand online service for lesbian newbie, asking her if she had chicken out on her again.

"No Mindy, Bailey said. I'm outside; just give me a moment to gather myself together. You just get a table and order me a Bellini or Mimosa please; I just have to return a phone call to my friend Johanna." It was a lie Bailey just needed more than a moment. In fact she had put the keys and started the ignition once again but turned it off and started that walk toward the door.

Just as Bailey summoned enough strength to go through the door, a woman walked up to the bar and she looked just as scared as Bailey felt. She just stood there as if she was wrestling with going in. Bailey walked over to her, recognized that deer in the headlights look and placed a hand on her shoulder for comfort. She looked into Bailey eyes with a pleading look for help so Bailey whispered two words. Let's go! They took off running and laughing hysterically, got into the car and Bailey sped off not knowing where she was headed. She drove straight ahead for a couple of miles until they reached a park. She parked the car and they both got out walked over to the snowball vendor; bought peach snow cones with a condense milk and whip cream topping and sat at the furthest bench from the stand.

Simultaneously as if they were holding their breath each exhaled and really looked at each other. A faint thank you came from this small woman who introduced herself as Tanja. Tanja Stoppings from Shreveport, La. Bailey introduce herself and even though the formalities was out of the way there still was the what just happen factor in the quiet air. Bailey broke the silence first by saying that she stupidly had a threesome with her boyfriend and even though he broke up with her for the other women, she still had a curious wanting to explore more with a woman. She told Tanja how she was supposed to be meeting this woman name Mindy that she met on the "Rainbow One Night Stand" website and how she had driven her car around and around the bar before deciding to go in. It was her first time going to a lesbian bar and she was scared out of her mind.

Tanja had a similar story except she followed her fiancée here to Ponde, Louisiana from Denim Springs, Alabama. They were involved in several threesomes and he too left her for the woman du juor. Of course he took off in her car but the good news is she still had a job and a place to live, even though she wasn't certain she would stay in Ponde, Louisiana much longer. Then Tanja told Bailey that she was glad she came along because she probably would have made a fool out of herself in the bar whereas she most likely would have gotten picked up by a big bush dyke with a tongue ring and tattoo, not what she was looking for.

Where do we go from here Bailey wondered as if Tanja was reading her mind said those exact same words out loud. Again the laughter began. Once they recovered there was a mutual decision to take things slow as they exchanged phone numbers and if things progress then so be it and if they don't maybe a good friendship can be had. Only in Bailey mind she was thinking she had enough friends with Airis, Chandenise, Kya and Johanna (a woman she bonded with at a swingers club) she was looking to cure the longing she had for the touch of a woman.

Bailey asked Tanja where could she drop her to and they drove off with small talk and sideways glances at each other. Before getting out of the car Tanja leaned over and kissed Bailey on the cheek, thanked her again and sauntered into her apartment building leaving a confused Bailey even more bewildered.

The phone ringing brought Bailey out of her static shock. She reached into her purse to see who was calling and it was Johanna, the one bff who she told all her darkest secrets as well as the only one who knew what she was up tonight. Bailey answered the phone with a sly smile. "Hello Jo, You're never going to believe what happen Bailey said." Before starting the car she placed her Bluetooth into her ear and relayed the whole scenario of the night as she drove home.

Once inside Bailey went straight to the bathroom and started her Jacuzzi tub. She again played the incident over and over in her head while soaking neck deep in the hot spraying water. She couldn't get the way Tanja looked out of her head. She hated keeping secrets from her BACK associates but they wouldn't understand, especially that man-nizer Chandenise.

Now out of the tub, Bailey laid across the bed remembering how stupid she was in giving into a man again. She should've learned from her experience in high school but Bailey thought she was so in love with Derrick and the sex was phenomenal. They used sex toys, food, made videos and played sex games but soon that wasn't enough for Derrick. He made the suggestion of doing a threesome. Bailey was reluctant at first but gave in like so many women thinking this would keep her man.

Her name was Aldonza, and they picked her up at club called Monarchs. The plan was to get in, mingle and pick out a prospect. Aldonza was the fourth woman that Bailey and Derrick entertained the idea with. Oh they didn't come out and directly ask for a threesome. They just sat down and talk to women to see if the chemistry was right. Both had to attract to the women in order for the threesome to work.

Derrick was excited at the thought of seeing the two of them together as well as the three of them. He talked about it, hinted about and just plain got on Baileys nerve for months. Finally a couple of months before he walked out on her, they did the deed. It wasn't as uncomfortable as Baily thought it would be. In fact, it seemed second nature.

It started off once a month, twice a month then next thing Bailey knew three to four times a week. Bailey enjoyed Aldonza's touch and the way Derrick eyes lit up when he watch the two women together. Bailey sometimes found herself looking at her friends in wonderment of how they could turn her completely on and then find comfort in resolving those feelings by masturbating.

Kya almost caught her once. They were on one of their B*A*CK excursions to a Mississippi casino. Bailey had just finish swimming with her friends' pool sides when she became turned on by watching the girls play water volleyball with the other guest at the hotel. She told everyone she wasn't feeling well and went up to her room.

Jumping into a cold shower didn't do anything but stimulate Bailey even more, so she sat in the picture window of her hotel room, watch the water glisten off her friends bodies as their breasts and asses move with sexual vibration. She needed relief so she placed a towel under her in the chair and stroked her female button as she thought of all the ways they could satisfy each other.

Bailey was just reaching her climatic point and calling out how she wanted to lick Airis pussy when there was a knock at her hotel door. Fumbling around in embarrassment and hoping whoever was on the other side of the door didn't hear what just took place she grabbed her robe, took a deep breath and opened the door. There stood Kya with this strange look on her face; she didn't say anything she just back up and walked away toward her room down the hall. After that day Bailey noticed Kya was friendly with her but stood at a distance.

Now she was alone and cursing Derrick and Aldonza for messing up her life. Bailey knew her part in the situation was willingly but she hadn't figured out what to do about it. So she decided to pursue the woman thing in secret only sharing with Johanna because she was fighting the same demon. Bailey and Johanna tried the couple's thing but they were too much alike; they decided to be each other's support system and friends.

The next day Bailey picked up the phone and called Tanja. They talked an hour before Tanja invited Bailey over to her house and she accepted. Tanja's house was beautifully decorated with various hues of greens and browns with lots of plants but the kitchen was the grand prize. The walls were painted a gun metal color with plenty of shiny black cabinets along with stainless steel appliances. As the music of "Kem" played on the CD player they prepared a dinner of fried chicken, sauté green beans and mash potatoes and sat out on Tanja's patio while they ate and talked. It was a nervous conversation yet needed. In the end they decided that neither would be considered the manly one or maybe classify themselves as lesbian period; just two women who enjoy the pleasures of one another.

It's been two and a half years now and Bailey seems to be juggling her new life style and her friends' just fine. Occasionally she has to refer her lover Tanja as a he when the girls are together man bashing. Once or twice to keep up appearances Bailey and Tanja both went out on several blind dates set up by each other friends. Things were going so great that Bailey started subscribing to the rule of don't ask, don't tell.

Airis Uprising

Ya-Ya pick up the phone, oh Lord Lordly Lord! Kya looked over to the left wall where her answering machine stood then further upward toward the window seeing the moon was still smiling, turned over and went back to sleep. Rinnnnng! Rinnnnng! "Damn! Why Airis is calling me at four nineteen in the morning. Hello!" Kya said stumbling around her pillows and over Poodles, her pet Yorkie makeshift bed to answer the phone. Ya-Ya please help me I'm not sure where I am at but the police have got the place surrounded and also blocked off the streets.

"Air; don't you know what time it is?" replied Kya. "Yes, remarked Airis, but I didn't know who else to call. Shaun needed me to pick him up and Oh! Shit! POW! POW! Ahh! Wait a minute!" By then Kya sprung out of bed and over to her nightstand to turn on the light. Hello! Hello! Suddenly all Kya could hear was what seemed like a big crash with fumbling sounds there after Airis returned breathless to the phone, begging Kya to come and get her. Airis was one of Kya's girls so she had to help her. As Kya groggily drove her way to the rescue she wonder what happen to her friend because Airis was good when it came to playing the boys in high school but when it came to men she was as green as an unripe tomato.

The one thing that Chandenise was always instilling in the groups head was men were just boys with bigger heads, egos, toys and hopefully dicks but for some reason Airis always seems to get hooked up with what we call flaggers. Flaggers are the guys that when you first meet them it's all good but by some turn of event they said or did something that raises the hairs on the back of your necks cuing that something was wrong. Hence, rising of a flag!

Airis had blinders on for that type. She would meet so and so, the group wouldn't see or hear from her for about two weeks then by the third or fourth week she would call crying that whoever was the latest flagger at that present time didn't show or call. That usually meant the bastard had gotten what he wanted and its over or she was initially intended for kindling. Yet in Airis mind things were progressing, she had all kinds of excuse of why she couldn't get in touch with whatever flagger that was on her menu at that moment.

There had been many discussions among BACK where we have all tried to figure out when it all started and came to the conclusion that it had to back in Airis second or third semester of college because by the end high school let's just say we as a group had a game plan of destruction and stuck to it. In fact shortly after forming BACK Airis first victim was Raymond, a good looking varsity hunk with a three day a week part-time job and well to do parents. As recollection served Kya correctly; Airis met him on their first day of school at Ponde High during lunch time.

Raymond, Terrion and Stephen would come over to the tree almost every day trying to flex some male charm. Raymond smiled at Airis, and she took a "let's test the waters" interest while Chandenise and Kya played snooty hard to get girls. He walked Airis to her class after lunch and by the weekend they were a couple going shopping, movies and hanging out, but by that following Tuesday she was avoiding him and by that next weekend it was finite. To assure that it was over; Airis started the rumor that she just used him for his money and her practice pussy licker. Poor Raymond he was so distraught that his grades started slipping to the point a tutor was needed to academically keep his football status.

Next it was Fisher, Robert and so forth and Airis would use them and dropped them without batting an eyelash. Some didn't care because they knew her reputation and just wanted the sex and other thought she really cared about them; then there was an occasional suitor that dropped her first committing her into a seething oath that the next would pay for the sin. One poor guy she actually talked to him one week ahead of time just to get invited to an annual party and dumped him as soon as she set foot in the door to prowl around for the next victim. Thing pretty much went that way with her, until sometime during college.

Bailey, Chandenise and Kya decide to attend Ponde University and Airis drove ten miles to and fro to attend Wright University because their Culinary Arts program had a hands down reputation. Ponde offered the best in Accounting which Kya was majoring in, Bailey had a handle on majoring in Journalism and Chandenise was contemplating nursing and this Tuesday would be everyone in the group first semester. BACK decided to only meet on Fridays so they could take their studies seriously.

This particular Friday they were to meet at Chandenise for White Russians, movies and pampering. Airis being the treasure of BACK, made a stop after her last evening class to the local Deli & Everything Galore for some milk. Big mistake! She met Byron. Kya guessed he talked a good game because they exchanged cell numbers. Here is where the red flag comes into play. The brother calls her as she was leaving the parking lot and talked to her almost the entire time she was at Chandie's house. Judging from the Airis side of the conversation it appeared he was talking marriage and love at first sight. Come on yawl to eager, RED FLAG!

They talked Saturday, Sunday and Monday, by Wednesday a beautiful relationship was formed the kind that Airis like; wine, dine and shopping. Airis had invited Byron over for a candlelight dinner that Friday. He had a meal, took off his socks and shoes; four months later she had finally gotten rid of him. Byron reasoning for staying was he felt Airis owed him; he had been stealing from his mom to keep her happy. His mom final straw with him was when he started stealing her money and she threw him out. Coincidentally the day of the dinner invite Byron was riding the couch over at his sister's home and had just been thrown out of there that morning by his sister's husband.

Byron brother-in-law Rudy was tired of him lying there on the sofa bed when he rose to go to work and still lying there loafing when he came home at night, especially since Byron was just sitting there when his fourteen month old son RJ was playing around the TV and it fell on his poor little body and broke his right leg and foot. Airis rolled right along from Byron to Michael the porn fanatic, James the drug dealer that traded her car for drugs transporting, some skinny white guy name Nicholas that belittled her in front of his white friends and a few other flaggers that are now a blur and now Shaun.

The good thing about Shaun was that he was in college, had his own car and possibly had a future. Airis meet him in English class and the cycle started again. He would invite her for evenings out and conveniently forgetting his wallet. One time it was dinner and movie where she paid for the meal, they manage to make it outside of the theatre whereas he got a call, excused him to and left her there with no tickets, no nothing. She had to call Bailey to call to bring her home because she spent her money on dinner. He would imposed on her to throw parties at her apartment citing he lived at home with his mom and the clicker was the strange packages that would mysteriously appear in her mail box and she wasn't allowed to inquire about or even open.

There was some mystery to Shaun though but not in a good way. He was moody one minute and nice the next. Hence, the problem now, this jackass, you all forgive me for saying that but Airis got out of her bed at two a.m. to pick a man she just met twelve days ago to bring him to his alleged aunt's home and for what? As Kya pulled up to where the commotion was she spotted Airis sitting on the curb crying and watching her car being loaded onto a tow truck.

"Airis Paige Johnston!" Kya yelled when she got in the car, "What the hell was so important to this man that it couldn't wait for another four or five hours and some fucking daylight?" Airis started bawling and shaking so uncontrollably that Kya pulled the car over to comfort her friend. "He needed to get some money from his aunt to put gas in his car for the commute back and forth to school for the week. I didn't have it to give so he called his aunt. I offered to bring him in later in the morning but he kept calling and pestering me to pick him up so I did and waited forty nine minutes then mayhem struck!" revealed Airis.

Kya replayed "so you drove to Sellback, an unfamiliar and drug infested part of town, waited in the car for about hour in the dark, and shortly afterwards the cops came to raid the place! So did he get the money and where is Shaun now?" Airis slumped over onto the dashboard and said "the police found Shaun having sex with his so called aunt with cocaine trace around his nose. I know I know Karma is a bitch, right?"

Chandenise, one less secret!

———✎

It was spring break and BACK decided to get out of boring old Ponde, Louisiana and head to New Orleans. On the three hour ride there we played games like name the driver; guessing how the person may look judging by their car and make a word or phrase with the license number. Bailey got bored quickly with those games and wanted to play truth or dare, which didn't last long either because nobody wanted to play fair.

Pulling up to Chandie grandmother old ninth ward house, you could still see the markings from the guardsmen that told how many fatalities were inside after hurricane Katrina struck. Several piles of rubble that once were homes and across the street attached to a pole, a worn hanging sign that read "Welcome to Bunny Frances Park." We pulled into the drive way and a person wearing knee highs, slippers, and a house coat that had safety pins holding up the pocket appeared.

She greeted us at the door smoking a joint. "Oh Nana Rose," Chandenise said. "Aren't you too old to be still smoking weed?" Nana Rose froze in her track, stretch possibly to the height she once was, with hand on hips and said "As long as the deed to the house on Desire and France is in my name I will do what I want," turned and stomped away.

Grandma Rose was a smaller version of Chandenise, had that spitfire attitude and equally matching smart mouth. She said I know you gals should be hungry from your trip so I made a big pot of red beans and rice, potato salad, fried chicken and my special tropical punch koolade, but if you're going to spend your time nagging me about my habits you can make your plates to go.

Airis sat down at the table to get her grub on saying "yawl can go if you want to but the food smell so good," and poured her a big glass of the special koolade. Chandenise tried to warn her not to drink it but before she could finish getting the words out Airis had taken a great big gulp. Her eyes seemed to bugle out of her head and she proceeded to spew the red drink all over the floor. Nana Rose just laugh and said I'm late the criminal already have a head start.

Nana Rose grabbed a beer from the fridge and strutted to the porch. She had the best seat on the block to see the comings and goings around the neighborhood. If you wanted to know who did what, where and when Nana Rose was the tattler to go to. She sat on the porch with a beer, stern look and gave you that I see you and I'm telling look. Everybody knew if you wanted to commit a crime during the day you only had an hour to do it because between eleven and noon the "Young and Restless" occupied her attention and she retired inside every night at ten to catch channel "4 wwl "news, drank another beer and off to bed.

She was the first person TV reporters sorted out if a crime went down. Nana Rose would put on her TV house coat and flash her pearly white teeth; one of the fronts was trimmed in gold and had a champagne glass in the middle. She called it a memento from her "pussy popping" wild days. She felt it was her duty to look good on TV while telling all. This evening by the time she made it to her perch there was a scream for help. We all ran from the kitchen to see what the commotion was; someone just shot Billy. Nana Rose said I knew sooner or later Billy was going to get it, always creeping over there with Tandy. She is married has two children with a nice husband that goes to work every day and she wants to lay up with that bum.

"Billy who" Chandie ask. "You know that no good black ass ex of yours," Nana replied. Shhh! Nana! Chandenise said slapping her hand across her grandmother's mouth cutting her words off. "Chandenise, Nana said please don't tell me after all these years you still have feeling for that dead beat?" Chandenise replied "hell no, but the other thing is a secret and I would like to keep it that way." For some reason that statement enraged Nana Rose, she looked Chandenise square in the eye and said you can't run from your past. It will catch up with you sooner or later.

Before the police arrived Chandenise walked over to look at Billy's bullet riddled body, gave a deep throated hawking, spat on him and walked away with a tear streamed face. She couldn't believe the dead man was the same person that she ran away with to Little Rock, AR, got her pregnant and dumped her. Leaving her in a strange state with no family or friends, broke and alone, having her to crawled back home to New Orleans with her tail between her legs.

Chandenise lived with her mother Lois and Nana Rose during her pregnancy. She was so ashamed of her situation that she dropped out of school and made a mental promise to never fall for a pretty boy ever again. After baby girl Kenya was born, Chandenise mother decide that they would be better off with a fresh start in another city so they packed up, moved to Ponde and forget that they are a part of the prominent Tyler family of New Orleans.

Lois played the part of a single mother of two. Chandenise played the part of a rebellious teenager repeating the ninth grade. She never thought of Kenya as her daughter. Lois did everything for the baby. Doctor's appointments, diaper changes, birthday celebration, the works. When Lois told her daughter to forget that she have a baby, Chandenise took it literally.

Chandie went right on thru the last year of junior high and high school on the fast track. She dated, mated and dumped boys after boys. Her taste of the horizontal slow ride grew. She kept female friends at bay until her cousin Airis and her family moved to Ponde. Then things really got wild. Sneaking out to party at the local hang out spot, alcohol, drugs and sex played a humongous part in her life. Until one day during a routine gynecologist visit she was diagnose with herpes.

Chandie managed to keep motherhood from Airis because she lived in Charlotte, NC at the time her of pregnancy and now this new revaluation of having an STD. She couldn't tell her cousin and definitely not her mother bringing more shame upon her, especially in her uncle's eyes. Airis father, Lois brother, always thought of his sister as a fast one. Getting pregnant again and not knowing who the father was is a deadly sin! He called her careless for having unprotected sex knowing that AIDS killed their younger sister Monica. Lois was determined to protect her daughter and continued the charade.

Chandie was able to forget the past during recent visits to New Orleans but now with Billy's lifeless body in front of her; those painful memories are back in full force. Scanning his body one last time she could see the healed deep gash on his left shoulder. He received that cut trying to sell baking soda as cocaine to a young drug user and the brush burn scars she gave him during an argument where he slapped her cutting her left jaw with a ring. They were living in different motels every week and money was real thin. He wanted her work the pole at the local strip club or start strolling up and down University Street like the locals. Billy figured it was fast money until he could get a job working at the local dairy plant.

One day he pulled into the car wash and pointed out which woman was selling herself and suggested that Chandenise try. He got out of the car and started talking to a group of men. The scraggily man with the egg size knot on his forehead started grinning as Billy whispered something in his ear and the man gave Billy some money. As they turn to approach her, Chandenise jumped into the car peeling off fast. She hadn't notice Billy or his shirt caught in the door until she had drugged him quite a few inches across the traffic lights of University and Ashner Avenue.

The ride back home to Ponde was even longer than the drive there. Airis, Bailey and Kya (BACK) were all trying to figure out why Chandenise tears flowed so heavy. She broke down and told them the story of how she thought she was in love with Billy, and how he convinced her at fifteen to leave with him to Arkansas. How when she told him a year later she was pregnant he disowned her and left her destitute. Also, Chandenise revealed that three and a half year girl everybody thinks is her little sister is really her daughter. They rode the rest of the way home, in silence.

So now Chandenise will take only one secret to her grave!

19

Kya's Aftermath

T he ambulance and police has now arrived on the scene. Kya's thinking was quickly snapped back from the past to the present once the attendant placed a cold ice pack to her lumpy head. She looked over at the poor gentlemen that got shot for his part in something he had no knowledge of as he was being loaded into the back of the emergency vehicle. He still has that puzzle look on his face and who could blame him. He thought he was coming over to get his grub on and perhaps mack on a pretty lady at the same time instead he got chased by a manic with a gun.

Bruce in the meantime has just realized the signification of what he just did as the police officer cuffed and mirandize him. He has gone from being enraged with jealousy to staring blankly into space as he was being led from the kitchen toward the door. He glanced down at his handy work laying there with her neck cut and broke into tears. As the police carted him pass Kya he mouth the words "I'm sorry", dropped his head down and didn't resist being led into the police car.

Kya walked over to the spot where her dear friend body laid cold on the floor. Her eyes were open but even in death she had this smirk air about her. As if to say as I'm still hot stuff and I'll go to my grave with it. Tears started to flow as she knelt to shut her friend's eyes but she had to get herself together so she can be there to console Lois, Kenya and Nana Rose. Oh goodness Kya thought who is going to tell this feisty old woman that her granddaughter was dead.

Kya dialed Airis number and soon as she answered she shout she dead. Airis! Chandenise is dead! Bruce is arrested for killing her and attempting to kill her boyfriend. I'm here waiting on the coroner. Call Bailey and you guys get here. Hanging up Kya dialed Lois cell phone, told her to have a seat and then relayed the gruesome news. There was nothing but silence on the other end of the phone but one of Lois's co-worker and friend pick up her cell identified herself as Mary and said Lois passed out.

Since Kya knew Mary was on of Lois's friends she told her what happen. Mary promised to get Lois to the hospital morgue and suggested that Kya go pick up Kenya from Lois's house. Oh my goodness Kya hadn't thought about that. She didn't want the little Kenya to hear the bad news from someone else but she also didn't want to leave her friend lying there. She dialed Airis again and asked her to pick up Kenya and go straight to the hospital.

Bailey arrived about the same time as coroner. She just stood there with her mouth wide open as she surveyed the destruction of the house and once she spotted Chandenise body she fell to her knees and wept. The only coherent thing Kya could make out as to what Bailey was saying were the words what happened. They watched in dismay as the coroner stab some type of instrument into the body, made a notation on a clipboard and then the coroner along with her helper pick Chandenise's body up, rolled her into a black bag, zipped it and carted her away.

By the time Airis made to the house, Bailey and Kya were just sitting there staring into space. No one wanted to speak; they just sat there mimicking a rocking chair. They all damn near jumped out of their skin when Chandenise cell phone, still sitting in the spot where her bloody lifeless body once lay rang. "Somebody answer the damn phone!" Bailey shouted.

It felt too eerie to pick up her friends phone but Kya answered the phone anyway to the cursing of Nana Rose. She was demanding that Kya put Chandenise on the phone and stop playing this mean and cruel joke after Kya told her the bad news. She said enough is enough and she wanted to speak to her granddaughter. Kya was sure

Nana Rose was high and given the news she wasn't in the reasoning mood.

"Nana Rose", Kya said "I'm sorry but Chandenise is dead. Bruce killed her". Kya had to put the phone down because the old lady was yelling and sobbing hard, yet again screaming what happen? Kya told what she knew and how she was invite to a barbeque but by the time she got there the destruction had already started. She also told Nana Rose how Bruce shot up the house, guess house and a stranger that was visiting. She didn't have all of the details of what happen but she was one hundred percent sure Chandenise was dead and Bruce was her killer.

Nana Rose told Kya she would be on the next grey hound bus smoking and to make sure someone had their ass there to get her and hung up. Bailey spoke and said "We need to get this place together before Lois and Kenya get here. I know it will be hard but if there ever was a time for B*A*C*K to come together and be strong now is it. What happen was tragic but we all know Chandenise was happy doing what she does best and that's stringing along men and playing a brother. Oh yeah and simply being in charge—of everything"

Airis commented that she was surprise when Chandenise decided to marry Bruce. Airis also said she thought Chandenise player days was over but when she ran into her a couple of weeks ago at Mary's Eatery she was chowing down with Benson Martin. Bailey asked "wasn't he a teammate of Bruce"? Airis replied "yes he was a former New Orleans Warrior pro football player but now he is a politician. When I spoke with her later that night she said she and Bruce had separated three weeks earlier because the woman Bruce was having an affair with called the house to say she was pregnant". Kya damn nearly dropped the bucket of soapy water she was carrying to mop the blood up off the floor with. She really couldn't believe what she was hearing.

"You must be mistaken" Kya said to Airis "are you sure you heard Chandenise correctly"? Airis nodded with a yes motion then continue the conversation by saying my cousin said Bruce confirmed the pregnancy himself and walked out on her saying he never should have married a tramp like her in the first place. That's why she bought the new house without him, filed for a separation and went on a wild spending spree for herself and Kenya making sure they had everything they needed and a few things they wanted. Chandenise swore me to secrecy because she was too embarrassed to let anyone know that while she had given up her wild ways she got played in the end.

Airis had to be wrong Kya was thinking this was so over whelming to her that she just started crying, everyone thought it was because of the recent death. Her two friends rushed to her side. There they stood in a group of hugs, cries and sobs but Kya's cries were for something else.

Something she couldn't tell and hope no one would found out so for as far as Airis and Bailey was concern her tears were for Chandenise but she did intend to investigate matter further as soon as all the grieving was over. She thought she knew Bruce they talked about any and everything; well Kya chuckled I guess not everything since a baby would soon be born and it was the first she heard of it.

The trio had just finish cleaning up all the blood stains and put what furniture and stuff they could back in place when Lois and Kenya arrived. Kenya ran straight up to her room while Lois just perched on the arm of the sofa. She thanked the girls for tidying up before they arrived. She said she told Kenya that mommy went to heaven to play with the angels. She believes she understood for a child of almost eight years old. Lois additionally said she was taking Kenya back to her place and for them to lock up and they would discuss things in the morning.

Kenya arrived back downstairs with her suit case pack. She looked as if she had had a good cry. She glanced over at a picture on the coffee table of the woman she had recently come to know as her mom. With her two front teeth missing at the top she smiled and said "my mommy was beautiful so don't worry the angels will take good care of her and she will be looking down on all of us from heaven". Kya silently prayed that wasn't true because she would have some explaining to do and knowing Chandenise she would come back and haunt her as payback.

With the house locked tight, Bailey suggested they all go get something to eat. At the time it was a good idea but once they made it to Grady's eatery, everyone appetite seemed to diminish. They decided to order drinks instead. Kya's mind was somewhere else as they started reminisced about Chandenise. She just hummed and nodded at what was being said. She needed to get away, away to think about what Airis said about a pregnant woman.

Who could it be and why didn't Bruce say anything to her about it, hell they talked about everything else her mind kept replying. She wonder was she just another hen passing through Bruce's rooster house or could it be he really did want to be with her and that they found each other too late as he would always say to her with a kiss. No the best thing for her to do was to go home and think about the indirect part she played in her best friend's death.

They got it started

Finally home and alone, Kya didn't even bother to turn on the lights. She just walked over to her answering machine to check her message. You have one new message and one saved message the woman on the machine said. Beep—New message today: Ya-Ya! It's me, come on baby pick up, this is my one call and I had to call you. Kya deleted that message before it finished. Friday May 27—hey girl, what's up, got a que going on tomorrow and I know how you like my bbq sauce. Come on by, got a friend I want you to meet.

It was one of the last words from one of her best friend welcoming her to partake in good food. The flood gates open again. Kya just balled up on the sofa and cried her eyes out. How could Bruce cheat on Chandenise? Better yet how could she do something like that to her friend? To cheat with Bruce was one thing Kya thought but he was also cheating on her with someone else and she was pregnant. It was a mistake, a big huge mistake that started with one drink too many at a bar seven or eight months ago at a time when she was really, really lonely.

Grayfish Tavern, on a Saturday night, Kya was stood up for dinner for what seem like the hundredth time that year, so she drove over to Cisco bar to have a few drinks. Bruce was in there with a few of his co-workers. They invited her to their table and the spirits flowed freely. Kya was enjoying all the manly attention that she totally forgot that Erik never showed up for dinner. In fact she enjoyed herself so much that she couldn't drive home. So when

Bruce offered to drive her there she poured herself into the passenger side of her car, tossed him the keys and closed her eyes for the ride.

Bruce on the other hand had other ideas. As he drove Kya home he took assessment of her body. She was wearing a pretty pink v-cut dress the showed the rise and fall of her beautiful chocolate breast. He had already admired her body from afar and when the car stopped at a red light he gently brushed his fingers along her cleavage. Kya's moaning response triggered a response in his pants and Bruce knew he shouldn't be doing something like that but he also knew he would probably never get another chance like this one again. He was banking on the fact that Kya would be so embarrass by her drunken behavior that she would keep what happen between the two of them, so tonight's motive was to hit it and quit his fantasy.

Kya remembered Bruce helping her inside to the sofa and saying something about heading to the kitchen. As he put on a pot coffee as she turned on the radio. "Let's get closer" by Atlantic Starr was just coming on the air. Kya began swaying her hips to the smooth mellow music while Bruce watched her from the kitchen. By the time the coffee was ready Kya had kicked off her shoes and was enjoying "In between the sheets" by the Isley Brothers. Bruce handed her the coffee and sat down to watch as she continued to dance.

She sauntered over to the mirror that hung over the mantelpiece. While looking at her image Kya asked Bruce "what was wrong with her? Why couldn't she keep a man? Was it her looks"? Bruce just stated that perhaps she scare men with her beauty. He said some men are scared of a woman that has beauty and brains. I for one am not. As he said those words he was standing so close behind Kya that she could not only feel his manhood rising but the smell of it was intoxicating to her and now they were staring in each other's eyes through the mirror.

"Kya you're so beautiful, Bruce exclaimed "sometimes I wish I would've meet you first. You have your act together and a brother would have to be crazy not to see that you're a good woman". He started gliding his fingers up and down her arms as he blew on the nape of her neck, then his tongue began to trace the rim of her ear as he slow grind on her round plush ass. His strong manicured hands came around and grabbed her breast causing Kya to exhale a gust of wind that would've blown out a burning house. Bruce turned her slowly toward him, dropped to his knees to search for the chocolate mound underneath the pink wrapping and like a lizard's darting tongue of quick acute movement, hit his target. Kya knew she shouldn't be letting him do it, but she was drunk and it felt so good. He picked her up and carried her to the bedroom and the wrong deed began.

Bruce called her the next day. He said he told Chandenise about running into her at the bar, bringing her home and once he got her inside he called a cab and headed back to the bar to his car. He also let Kya know that he wanted to see her again and couldn't wait until tonight when they all go out to dinner. "Oh yeah," Bruce remarked "wear something short and sexy baby. That's how I want to remember you when I go sleep tonight." Kya was amuse as she hung up the phone and ran straight to the closet like a little school girl to pick out her wardrobe.

It was a weekly dinner that was kept by Kya, Bruce and Chandenise. Sometimes Airis or Bailey and their dates would join along with whatever gentleman the gang was trying to fix Kya up with. On this night it was Michael Curtain. He was tall, successful and handsome but Kya had her eyes on Bruce. He was sitting there wearing a pair of loose fitting blue jeans, with a light blue low turtleneck shirt, diamond bling in his ears, neck and wrist, smelling of cool water cologne and exerting the look of sex and money. She made small talk with Michael while sitting in between him and Bruce but once Bruce started methodically rubbing her thighs underneath the table she excused herself and went to the bathroom to splash some cold water on her face.

In the bathroom she placed both palms on the sink and just sunk her head down. She couldn't believe she was doing this with her best friend's husband. She raised her head to look in the mirror, turned on the faucet to splash the cold water when suddenly she was shoved into the bathroom stall. It was Bruce and he was fully loaded with an erection. She simply stood on her tip toes, thanked herself for not wear any panties and let Bruce have his way. He entered her womanhood with quick precision and banged her good in what seemed like a few minutes. Breathlessly, he whispered "I couldn't wait and that will have to hold me until Monday night". Then he bent down suck her already hard nipples through her dress, zipped his pants and out the door and into the men's room across the way.

By the time Kya made it back to the table Bruce was already seated and talking politics with Michael. Chandenise had a puzzle look on her face so Kya made up the excuse that it must've been something she ate at lunch that had her stomach upset but she was ok to continue with dinner. To keep up with the façade of an upset stomach Kya told Chandenise she was going to eat light, so instead of ordering a big juicy steak that this restaurant was famous for, she ordered a small chicken chef salad and an ice tea. Kya almost choked on her salad when Chandenise made a funny comment about the wet stain area of the nipple on her dress, Kya just laughed it off by saying it must've happen when she splashed water on her face.

After dinner the group went dancing at Two Steps one of the most famous dance clubs in Ponde. Whenever celebrities visit the city, Two Steps was the spot they went to. It had two huge dance floors, intimate tables, great food and a secluded VIP section. Of course, being with Bruce England, an ex-football star and a famous lawyer in Ponde and his wife Chandenise a socialite, you were destined to be VIP where ever you go. The music was a great mixture of old school and today's r&b and everyone was having a great time on the dance floor all the way up to last call.

Michael drove Kya home and they made plans to see one other again the upcoming weekend. She thanked him for a good time and headed inside to look at her cell phone which had be vibrating with text messages from Bruce since they left the club. One message said how beautiful and graceful she looked on the dance floor, one said he couldn't wait to see her again and the last one gave details on what he was going to do with her Monday night, that one sent tingles to her woman cave. Then there was one from Chandenise telling her to be a naughty girl for once and give Michael some, maybe if she gets laid she wouldn't be so uptight and settle down. If Chandenise only knew she was getting laid by her husband, she would probably cut the brakes on her car or splash battery acid on her body like she did Galana Smith in high school when she caught her and her boyfriend Thomas kissing and nobody could prove it but Kya knew the truth.

On Monday morning when Kya arrived at work there were two bouquets sitting on her desk. A bouquet of a dozen yellow roses and the other bouquet were large beautiful white, yellow and pink calla lilies. Dylan, Kya co-worker said "somebody must've gotten lucky this weekend. Two bouquets of expensive flowers, girl you did something or someone right." Kya swatted at Dylan with her purse, smiled and made a bee line straight for the Lilies. Once she read the card and found out they came from Bruce she was grinning from ear to ear. It seems during their talks he paid more attention than she thought because they were her favorite flowers.

Later that morning Chandenise called Kya and invited her to lunch with her and Bailey. Chandenise wanted to get the juicy scoop on whether Kya like Michael or not. Kya opted not to go to lunch with the girls but instead eat her leftover dinner she towed for lunch at her desk. Just as she hung up the phone with Chandenise line two of her office phone rang. She assumed it was Bailey trying to convince her to come to lunch with her and Chandenise but it was Bruce; Hey beautiful meet me out back was all he said then he hung up. Kya was as giddy as a school girl, threw her pork chop back in the container, pulled her compact out of her purse to check her makeup and strutted toward the back door. Once outside she noticed Bruce had laid out a blanket on top of the rickety lunch table with a small picnic spread consisting of champagne, cheese, crackers and grapes. "It's not expensive and you are at work so one glass for you but isn't it romantic?" he asked as he reached out and grabbed Kya's hand leading her to her seat. Bruce added "Chandenise would never appreciate anything like this." Thus the beginning of a romance that never should be!

It has been three months of romance blitz for Kya with Bruce. Each time she is with him the whole world stops and they are the only two living on the planet. Kya had it so good that each time the group went out, double dated or just the girls hanging out; her jealousy of Chandenise ceased. She was secretly enjoying the benefits of lavish gifts as her, trips as her and more importantly her man. To ease her mind Kya sat down to write a letter to Chandenise but the phone rang and it was the very man she been thinking about all day. He was coming over for a brief stay because he just wanted to look into her bedroom eyes. Bruce would do and say little things like that to her and it made her feel very special. Kya did a second line dance to her bedroom to take a quick shower and put on a plum nightie and spritz on "Ralph Lauren Blue" perfume for an added effect of seduction. Hell he bought the stuff for her so she might as well flaunt them for him; secretly she wanted a little taste of his dick and a quickie would do just fine for now Kya thought as she step into a pair of heeled feathered plum slippers.

It's now the nearing March and Kya's 23rd birthday and she wanted to do something different for Bruce, she chuckled at the absurdity of because it her birthday and she is doing something for him but knowing Bruce as she does he will most definitely have something beautiful for her; especially since he went to New York for a weekend deposition with a sister law firm. Kya got an idea from a magazine she read in "Cosmopolitan" about seduction with saran wrap so on her lunch break she retrieve the magazine from the employee's lounge and re-read up on the art. Out of the three options she chose the easiest one of just simply wrapping yourself from breast to foot. Hell it was something she knew she couldn't possibly mess up; Kya couldn't wait to get off five o'clock.

A quick stop at the nearest Wal-Mart for some saran wrap Kya was on her way home and feeling real devilish. She had received a text from Bruce saying his plane will be touching down at five fifteen, he had to stop at the office real quick and he would be there around six thirty—six forty five depending on the traffic. That gave her time to set up the seduction scene. She added more candle to the existing ones all over the living room, bedroom and bathroom. Before her bath she set the CD player to play her favorite songs in succession. Now bathed and draped in a towel Kya lit all of the candles, sat down to apply her scented body butter and then began to wrap herself with the saran wrap. She started from her breast, down her body, ran into some trouble trying to cover her bountiful ass but after trial and error she succeed to be completely wrapped. As an added effect she poked a small hole around her left nipple and tied a stringed balloon around it that read "it's my birthday but I'm your present." It was a good thing she unlock the door and had the good sense to be close to the sofa because she couldn't move and she just heard Bruce car pull into her driveway.

Trying to strike a sexy pose in anticipation of Bruce, Kya propped herself aligned with the wall closet to the sofa, clicked the remote to the CD player and waited for the knock of her lover. The knock came in precisely twenty seconds later and she sweetly called out "come in sweetheart" and in walked the most beautiful things she had ever seen and the man presenting them wasn't bad either. Bruce was holding a Tiffany's box with a set of diamond earrings and matching necklace. For a brief moment Kya forgot about the tight clear wrapping around her body reach forward to receive the gift tumble, rolled and ended up lying between the sofa and coffee table knocking over the chilling bottle of champagne. Bruce yelped "Kya baby are you all right?" It took a few moments for him to realize why she couldn't move but once he did; he had to fight hard to hold in his laughter.

Bruce helped Kya off the floor by picking her up and plopping her down on the sofa. Kya was embarrassed and sweating from her plastic outfit." I'm sorry babe, I was trying to do something spontaneous but when I saw those diamonds I forgot for a moment that I was kind of restricted, well do you like it?" Kya asked. As he picked up the deflated balloon to read it Bruce began to show her how much he loved his gift for her birthday by unwrapping his present. He hovered over her slowly peeling each layer stopping to pay special attention to certain parts of her body and Kya released the snake charming it into attention with each downward upward stroke of her mouth and tongue. Now with the entire saran wrap gone and each of them turned on, Bruce lifted Kya up, motioned her to enclose her thighs around his neck bringing her impeccably sweet bald vagina lips to his lip and he stroked her clit almost into submission. Suddenly and slowly he slid her down onto his penis, Kya wrapped her legs around his six pack and clamped her hands on each shoulder; they stood there not moving but listening to "Don't disturb this groove" by "The System" with each feeling the other heartbeat. Still standing as one and saddle on Bruce's hardness, Kya arched all the way backward so that her palms were steady on the cushions of the sofa; letting Bruce take his cue from her move.

Now in the bedroom and it's almost midnight, Bruce got out of the bed to get the jewelry that he never had a chance to put on Kya. He walked back into the room and watched her sleep peacefully with a look of pure gratification on her face. Every rise and fall of her chest he realized that he was falling in love with Kya. She was everything Chandenise was and wasn't. She was glamorous, loved the small thing he did for her the most, enjoyed the time they shared together and unlike Chandenise appreciated the material things but didn't have her hand in his pocket. No Kya was different indeed he thought. Bruce sat on the bed and stroke Kya's hair gently so not to wake her. Then he regretfully noticed it was time for him to go home so he showered and dressed quietly, pulled the birthday card out of his jacket pocket, placed it on the night stand along with the Tiffany's box, leaned over and kiss Kya on her lips grabbed his keys to head home to his wife that will be looking for an enormous elaborate gift of some sort. He knew that he didn't have one and would probably end up sleeping in the guest room just to get a little sleep because Chandenise would be in full nagging bitch mode.

Kya woke up around three thirteen. She knew Bruce would be gone but she could help hoping that when she opened her eyes his gorgeous face would be nestled in the pillow next to her. "Oh shit, my back hurt!" Kya loudly said as she rose to go to the bathroom but she stopped in her tracks at the sight of the gift box from Tiffany's, she put on the necklace and earrings and wiggled her way to the toilet. While washing her hand she admired herself in the mirror then proceeded to give herself a stern talking to. "Now you know you can't be upset, you knew going into this ill-gotten relationship he was another's husband so just be grateful for whatever time you have with him, sure he is an awesome lover, great listener, handsome, fine, strong and has good taste so love him from afar if you must love him," Kya voiced as she once again glared at the jewelry she was sporting. She then turned off the bathroom light, snuggled back under the covers to sleep until it was time to get up and meet with the ladies for a day after birthday celebration.

A Rat revealed among them

Its trail day one for Bruce and Kya was wondering whether to show up with the rest of the girls, Nana Rose, Kenya and Lois. Kya knew she had to be there because Chandenise was one of her bff's, but she didn't want to be there to face the wrath of those very same people when the truth came out about the affair. She still wondered who the other woman was and if the pregnant heifer would show her face.

Bruce was being charged with capital murder and attempted murder and because he was being held without bail he was lead into court wearing a bright orange prison jumpsuit and handcuffs. He scanned the court room as he was being seated, spotted Kya and gave her pleading look. Kya felt somewhat guilty because he had called her some many times and even if she was home she just couldn't bring herself to talk to him and opted to let the answering machine take the message. Nope! Not after what they did she couldn't talk to him at all.

Kya looked around the courtroom to see if Bruce's other indulgence was there. She spotted two pregnant females and for some reasons couldn't picture either with Bruce. Candidate number one was a very thin black woman wearing big hooped earrings, an off the shoulder mid-drift shirt exposing her tattooed bundle with a pair of blue jeans and extra-long fingernails with what looked like mini gold hoops hanging on the ends. Candidate number two, a woman of mixed race wearing a blue dress so tight that her skin was beginning to look the same color but it had her bundle tightly nestled. These women were less than elegant and Bruce loved sophistication. So she turned her attention back to the trail with occasional glances at the two women.

Court adjourned for the day and the last thing Kya wanted to do was go to dinner with the group and discuss what happen but she had to keep the façade up. The group went to the nearby Wendy's that was in walking distance from the court house. Kya order a bacon cheese potato and a large ice tea but she blindly picked at her food. She couldn't stomach little Kenya talking about the woman she had just come to know as her mom for the last year or so. Everyone else pitched in their stories and fond memories of Chandenise as well. Once everyone finish eating and walked back to their cars Bailey ask Kya if she could spend the night at her place since it was closer than hers and she didn't want to be late for court the next day. Kya didn't want company but again she had to keep up appearances and agreed.

"Come on Kya, Bailey said. We can take this moment to catch up. You know we haven't actually had a chance to really talk in months. Are there any handsome men in your life or is Michael still wining and dining you?" Kya shook her head and said no, she mentioned she had been on a couple of dates since Michael but they were duds and not worth the time. Kya dare not tell Bailey how Bruce had taken her on romantic dates, shopping trips, bought her the diamond necklace and earring set she was just admiring and recently Atlantic City for a week, his wife thought he was at a conference in Texas and Kya told Chandenise she going to visit her sister in Missouri leaving the day before Bruce to overt suspicion.

Bailey hopped up on the breakfast aisle as she popped the tab on a coke a cola and said "let's have an old fashion BACK session; we can call Airis or just you and me." They phoned Airis but she was already asleep for the night so it was just the two of them. Kya made Bailey promise that the subject of the trail was off limits for the night. "That ok with me," Bailey said as hopped off the counter top and plopped down on the sofa. Besides I have something I need to tell you and you may not like it. Now Kya was listening because before then she barely heard a word Bailey said. Kya heart started racing real fast as she grabbed the bottle of wine and sat next to Bailey. In her mind she was thinking Bailey new the secret she had been carrying around for these past months." Ok Bailey let's hear it," as she held her breath in preparation of defense, but when Bailey said I'm gay, Kya burst into a roaring laughter.

"Well damn Kya it's not that funny". Bailey clamored "Where is your support or question or something other than laughter? I figured if I could tell anyone in our small little group it would be you, and you just laugh at me". Now Kya was laughing with relief that her secret was safe and as soon as she could gather up her bearings she told Bailey that she suspected as much since the Mississippi trip and that it was ok, she still loved her. "You knew and didn't say anything?" Bailey asked. Kya replied "hell Bailey I figured you were working things out and eventually say something. Besides it doesn't matter a friend is a friend." Bailey then told Kya the story of her quest with different women and the lengths of disguises she have to go through to protect her relationship until she was ready to tell the world.

Bailey wanted to know if anyone else in B*A*C*K knew and Kya said no. Heck Bailey you know Chandenise and her cousin Airis was to involve with themselves back then and now to notice anything other than using men for their money. The rest of the late night discussion between the two went well as they discussed Bailey's new sexual journey and Kya's alleged lack thereof while the music played and wine flowed. Bailey answered Kya silly questions about two sided dildos, male and female roles and the sixty-nine position in the gay community. The duo also talked about how amazed they were that Airis had gotten her love life together and was getting married next year to a doctor. That night was just what Kya needed to forgot about her what had her upset; at least until morning.

They next day found the pair asleep on the floor in front of the CD player as the telephone rang. Kya stood up to answer it as she said a silent prayer that it wasn't Bruce calling from prison again. Luckily it was Airis calling to see if they were coming to court because it was about to convene. All hell they were up so late that neither of them heard the alarm clock blaring loudly in Kya's bedroom. We will be there in about an hour, she hung up the phone, woke Bailey up and they began to race around like a chickens with their heads cut off showering and dressed in no time flat.

Just as Kya and Bailey arrived and took their seat on the third row; the prosecution had just called their last witness to the stand to wrap up their case before the defense was being their starting statements. Just as the gentleman Kya assumed was Chandenise boyfriend entered the witness stand, Bruce lean over and whispered something in his attorney ear. Then his attorney Mr. Slade asked to approach the bench. Judge Racan granted the defense and prosecution permission to approach and from what Kya could over hear was the defense wanted this witness label hostile because it was alleged that he was having an affair with the defendant wife and the judge said dutifully noted.

The gentleman was sworn in, and then asked to state his name and occupation. He said, "My name is Scott Meriwether and I am a private investigator with Eyes and Ears Investigation Service." Prosecuting attorney Mr. AdGene then asked Scott how he knew the defendant. Mr. Meriwether replied that he was hired by the defendant wife Mrs. Chandenise England to follow her husband around and report his infidelities; that's when it occurred to Kya that during their scuffle in the kitchen the day of Chandenise death the guy now on the stand called her by her sir name, doing all the drama she had pick up on that.

Mr. Meriwether said during his investigation he discovered Mr. England had two indiscretions. Mr. Meriwether also said he had been following Bruce for the past twelve months and reported to Mrs. England on a weekly basis. Prosecutor AdGene then asked the private investigator if any of the women he saw the defendant with was present in the court room now. Scott looked around the court room and simply said "yes sir I do".

The prosecutor then asked Mr. Meriwether to point them out. Scott said while pointing at the court room full of people, the pregnant young lady on the front row over in the corner wearing the blue dress is Ms. Grainger and the young lady wearing blue suit, sitting there third row center Ms. Martinley.

Truth of Consequences

K ya saw the whole room look over at the first row left and then slowly zeroed in on her. She just sat there looking around as if she wasn't the guilty party. Nana Rose turned around from her right front row seat to speak and what she said would make a sailor blush. Then as in a domino effect Lois, Airis, Bailey and little Kenya turn and gave Kya the evil eye. Kenya had the look of her mother when she was angry in those big brown seven and a half year old eyes.

The look in that child eyes made Kya bow her head and cry as she heard the prosecutor ask Mr. Meriwether about the day in question. He said Mrs. England and I met through a mutual friend at a luncheon, once she found out what I did for a living she retained my services because she had a strong suspicion that the late night work sessions and phone calls were more than just work related.

Again during my investigation it was discovered that Ms. Grainger suspect number one worked for Mr. England. One night during my survey I saw Mr. England who seemed intoxicated at the time leave together after what appeared to be an office party. I followed the two to and address that I now know as Ms. Grainger's apartment. Mr. Meriwether said he parked his car a block down and took a look inside the window to see them both kissing; at which this time he took a couple of photos and reported the next morning to Mrs. England. This appeared to be the only time Mr. England ever saw Ms. Grainger other than work.

Mr. Meriwether said Ms. England still wasn't convinced that her husband was innocent and had me to continue to follow him.

About a few months later I followed Mr. England to a bar named Ciscos. He entered with and appeared to be in the company of three other gentlemen. I clocked Ms. Martinley arriving around eleven p.m.; the two left together around three a.m. and I followed them to again to what is now I know as Ms. Martinley apartment. Mr. England left about two hours later. Mr. Meriwether then stated Mr. England returned to Cisco's for about a half hour then went home.

By this time Kya starting wishing she was "Jeannie or Bewitch" from the old television shows so she could disappear instantly. She hadn't realize she was involuntarily blinking her eyes and twitching her lips in a desperate attempt to get away until Nana Rose said "come on bitch you ain't Jeannie or Samantha, its recess time and you got some explaining to do." Then she walked off mumbling about Kya thinking she was some character on a TV show. Kya didn't dare move, not even to let Bailey who was sitting next to her pass by. She knew that there was nothing she could say to any of them, especially little Kenya that would justify what she did and Nana Rose probably wouldn't give her chance to say anything anyway.

Once court was back in session Mr. Meriwether was called back to the stand, he divulged all the dates, times and almost exact details of every tryst Kya and Bruce had. From the first luncheon, to dinner dates, to home visits and even the trip to Atlantic City. He also said on the day of the shooting he followed Mr. England to Ms. Martinley apartment where he brought her a dozen roses but only stay for fifteen minutes and in the meantime Mrs. England had invited me over with pictures and other evidence to confront Ms. Martinley with. Mr. England had arrived to the home about fifteen minutes before Ms. Martinley in a jealous rage. An argument ensued and Mrs. England asked Mr. England to leave. They started toward the door then the next thing I knew she dropped to the floor and he started shooting.

After the defense presented their short argument, the jury deliberated for two hours and found Bruce guilty of first degree murder and attempted murder. Judge Racan sentence Bruce to sixty years in the Ponde Department of Corrections and he was led away. Court adjourned and now Kya is scared; so scared that she actually wet her pantsuit. She starting wishing she was being led away too, far far away from what she will be in stored for once she walked her pissy ass through those double doors.

Nana Rose and Lois thought Bruce should've gotten the death penalty and voiced their opinion loudly about it. Nana Rose even went as far as to approach Ms. Grainger to inform her that she shouldn't get any starry eye idea about money for that bastard baby she was carrying as she, Lois and Kenya were leaving. Airis and Bailey looked and shook their head at Kya as they left the courtroom. Again leaving Kya sitting there to think how sorry and stupid she was for letting things get that far and now one of best friends was dead and the guy she had an affair with was in jail for her murder so that makes her guilty by association.

It felt like she was wearing scarlet veil with a big "A" across her face as she took the walk of shame on trebling legs down the court house stairs; she was wet and alone. She knew she would have to explain one day and ask each for forgives but from the stares of Nana Rose, little Kenya, Airis, Bailey and Lois; Kya figured that day wasn't today and that she wasn't wanted in the group anymore. Once she made it inside her car Kay said a silent thank you to God that Nana Rose didn't come and whip her ass like she threaten to do right before she scared the pregnant women half to death with her harsh words. She had always wanted to leave Ponde after the roar of Hurricane Katrina and now it seems this would be a good time for it.

On the drive out of town to Little Pebble Arkansas, Nana Rose last words kept replaying over and over in Kya head. She said that Kya was so fucking stupid that she didn't even realize that she was the live pig invited to the roast. While pulled into a quaint little gas station in Mississippi as Kya finish pumping the gas into the U-Haul rental truck the reality of Nana Rose words really hit her. "Oh that cunning Chandenise it wasn't just a barbeque," Kya smirked as she rode off into the direction of a new life, leaving her friends, lover and fond memories of their relationship behind locked in jail.

Prologue to a new Beginning

So visit your nearest Bank of Deposit today where it's more than just money, we care about our customers, the commercial said then it fades to black. The court bailiff turned off the television and rolled it back into the corner. The prosecuting attorney rose to state his argument. Ladies and gentleman of the jury I intend to prove that the defendant Kya Martinley was the master mind and knew of the scandalous crimes that was taking place in the bank and is not the innocent victim she proclaims to be; then it was Kya lawyer turn to speak but she didn't hear a word he said because things went blank.

It was the destructive Hurricane Katrina hitting the Gulf Coast along with the death of one of her good friends seven months later that sent Kya running from the small city of Ponde, Louisiana to Little Pebble, Arkansas seeking a new life. Kya was in desperate need of a job; as she walked into the "Bank of Deposit" to cash a check given to her by the Red Cross she spotted the sign saying now hiring, apply online. Kya conducted her business and drove straight home, knelt on her knees to pray and claim the job in the name of Jesus then plopped down at her computer to apply.

The truth be told, it hasn't been easy living here in Little Pebbles and on this Friday Kya just couldn't take calling the unemployment number to check in one more time. This would be one of many applications she has done online or at a business for employment in at least three weeks and she was having a server case of applicant let down blues; but Kya soon found out to be careful what you wish for because money is the root to all evil and so is a jealous woman. Things just weren't looking good for your girl.

Kya got the call on Monday to come down to the head office that following Wednesday to take a test which she passed with flying color but had to interview with the local branch manager the next day to seal the deal. She walked into the branch confident she could pull it off because she definitely had plenty of money handling experience and loved to provide quality customer services. Looking back Kya guesses her clue that something was a missed should have been when the manager looked her over with an approving roving eye.

His name was Byron Barrow, a fat, geeky looking fellow that seems to be setting up some type of appointment as Kya entered his office. He rose from the desk to shake her hand and instructed her to have a seat while he steps out to talk to one of his tellers. When he returned he pull out what seemed like a date book, scribble something down, closed it and said now Ms. Martinley why do you think your "Bank of Deposit" material. Kya explained her qualification and in returned he laid out what is to be expected if she was hired and he would be in touch either way.

Both stood and exchanged handshakes and he escorted her through the lobby. Kya remember hearing one of the female tellers mumbling something about her looks being a good addition to the bank and she left there with a smile on her face. As Kya drove away she got the call to start training in one week; that was quick she hadn't even made to the traffic light up the street. Your girl was elated!

Because she was attending college in the morning Kya elected to do her training from the one to six shift (classes will be ending by the time she report for work), and instead of two weeks it took four between having to take the cbt's (computerize bank training) courses and hands on coaching at an actual branch. Finally it was time to start working at the South Lowerline St branch of "Bank of Deposit N.A" on that Monday. She was ready and gun-ho, this was a chance to independently rebuild her life.

Ever heard of Murphy's Law? You know whatever can go will go wrong and Murphy had his hand into everything. That morning Kya showerhead broke in her walk in shower so she had to take a bird bath in the sink, then she tripped over her iron cord causing it to stop working. She had to resort to the olden days of heating the iron on the stove top and last but probably not least her car smoked all the way to the job. As she pulled into the bank's parking lot it died blocking the Lowerline street entrance. Not a good way to start your first day on the job. Mr. Barrow arrived and helped Kya push her car to the closest parking spot and then proceeded to shake his head as he walked past her to put his key into the bank's door.

Kya was introduced to her co-workers: Nykole Washington, the assistant branch manager; Juane' Banks, the head teller; and tellers Barbara Johnston and Dominicki Tootie. Next was the security guard, who worked there every day and seems to be a friend to all, Captain Marcus Lewis a former marine and police officers. After all the introductions she was given her codes, keys, and assigned a workstation. It was the drive-thru window where you service four lanes of customers.

After counting her till, it was time to open the bank. Kya's first customer was a regular and his transaction was an easy one, the next was a business customer who handed her several transactions to do which caused her to work a little slower and before you know it there was a backup of cars all the way to the street. Kya conjure up a smile to combat the ugly stares of the customers, took a deep breath and dove in. First lane one, lane two, lane three, back to lane one and then lane four; this went on for about twenty minutes. By the time the drive thru was clear, Kya felt as if she would need a muscle relaxer to straighten the permanent grin on her face and a little libation for a pick me up.

The first day was long and brutal for her but Kya held her own and even manage to balance her till on the first night. Now it was a question of how she was going to get home. Her car was still sitting in the parking lot and when she tried to start it, it just coughed, sputtered and smoke rose like a cloud. By this time Juane' came out to get in her car and offered Kya a ride home. So she locked up her Jeep Liberty and took Juane' up on the offer.

On the ride to Kya home they talked about past jobs, spouses and kids. Juane' told her that she was a widow and had to two preteens to care for and she had been working at the branch for three years. She said she had trouble making ends meet until she started going to the meetings, then quickly change the subject by asking Kya more about herself. Kya relayed a soft version of her journey to Little Pebble that ended when they reached her apartment building. Juane' gave Kya her phone number so she can call her in the morning for a ride. Kya thanked her profusely and headed to the elevator that led to the floor of her apartment.

The next few weeks went by fairly fast and Kya seemed to be catching on pretty good. Several nights while closing she heard her new coworkers complaining about the weekend coming. She was amazed because she had always enjoyed the weekend; Friday nights were for going out dancing or catching up on sleep, Saturday nights were for errand running, completing house cleaning and possibly two stepping on the dance floor and Sundays were for church and getting prepared for the upcoming work week. To Kya the weekend was a haven of relaxation no matter what!

One Wednesday during Kya's twelfth week on the job she overheard the ladies complaining yet again about the weekend. Barbara was saying to Dominicki that it was Juane' turns with Mr. Muscles and she wasn't too happy about it and wanted to switch dates with her. Dominicki just shrugged and said Juane' shouldn't worry about things, Nykole will be back from her vacation and we will discuss it at tonight's meeting. Again with the meeting, Kya thought.

Kya had heard at least fourteen or fifteen times about this so call meeting. She wondered was it bank related or some type of club they belong to. She was curious about the meeting so she nosily asked Juane' "What is this meeting you guys are always talking about?" Juane' squirmed at first then she asked Kya was today the end of her three month probationary period and when Kya replied yes all Juane' said was that she will be invited soon enough.

Just then as if he was eavesdropping, Mr. Barrow came out of his office and gave Juane' the evil eye as he walked thru the lobby and behind the teller line. He started asking Kya if she enjoyed dining out or dancing, her favorite type of music and if she had a boyfriend? Kya didn't think anything strange about the questions she figured he was trying to get to know her or just making conversation as they ended the day. She wanted to ask Juane more question on the way home but didn't want to make her feel even more uneasy, so instead they rode together singing in unison to R&B oldies.

On Thursday morning Kya was finally invited to a meeting. It was after work at Wally's, an expensive restaurant in the River Market area. Kya rode with Juane'; she was basically quite the whole time. Juane' only spoke to ask two questions that Kya considered very personal. She asked her how do she stand with money and if she would ever consider dating outside her race? It may seem like crazy questions but you'll find out why I asked.

They arrived the same times as Mr. Barrow, Barbara, and Dominicki and were seated at what seem like their normal table. George the waiter came over and asked if everyone wanted their usual drink and appetizers. He then turned to Kya and said "what will the newbie have?" Kya ordered a Wally punch and the cheesy sticks with ranch dipping sauce. George gave her a little smile and said be careful that punch packs a lot of punch young lady and then he walked away.

By the time the drinks arrived Nykole had joined the group and was talking about all the fun she had on her vacation to Jicama. She pulled out a shopping bag and started giving out the gifts she brought for everyone including Kya. After the entrees and another round of drinks, Mr. Barrows got real serious and announced that the meeting should start.

He went into his briefcase and pulled out four tangerine looking envelopes with the words Merry Ladies along with the employees name written on it and passed them around the table until each package made it to its name sake. Mr. Barrow looked at Kya and said "if you played her cards right you could have one next week." Kya watched in amazement as her coworkers counted their cash, folded the flap back and stuck in their purses as natural as breathing, which at this moment Kya was having a hard time doing.

"Now Nykole" Mr. Barrow announced, "Your expenses this week was a little more than normal so you owe the fund two dollars. Barbara and Dominicki you own the usual seventy-five and Ms. Juane' I haven't gotten an inventory on you this week but I suspect you have it with you." With a nod of her head Juane' reached into her purse and handed Mr. Barrow an orange colored invoice.

Ms. Kya, we invited you to give you a chance to join in and make a whole lot of cash. This involves going on dates, spending time with other people being their companion and nothing else. We cater to the rich, male and female and your cut would be tax free. We have weekly Thursday meetings where I give out salaries, talk of new clientele and basically adhere to the needs that are needed to maintain a good look and create a good time for our dates.

Then it was Nykole turn to talk. She announced that the way things works is that the Merry Ladies have arrangements with several hair salons, nail salons, massages therapy, a couple of boutiques and restaurants. It's all under a set price range and if you go over you have to pay the difference back into the business. This is where your stipend comes in; it allows for maintenances overage plus food and entertainment. These people are paying five hundred dollars to be entertained by Merry Ladies so don't be stingy or wasteful; just show the clients a good time and sit back to reap the rewards.

"I'm not a pimp and these are not my whores but I do maintain the books, screen and background our clientele, set up the dates via breakfast, lunch or dinner." Mr. Barrow said. My cut is minimum but lucrative. One of the main reasons I choose you to work with us is because you have the look our clienteles are going for. You're a little rough around the edges but with a little sprucing and wardrobe update you would fit right in.

"Kya we keep hearing you say you would like to return to college someday and we all know you can use a new set of wheels; you can earn enough to do that and more. Come on Mr. Barrow said I promise there is no sex involved." Kya couldn't say anything. She just sat there doing an overview of her fellow coworkers. They were all well dressed, latest wigs, tracks or hair style and driving nice cars; now to her the picture has become clear.

Once the dessert arrived, Kya just picked at hers, while others chatted and talked of the best place to get eye brows and bikini waxes, clothes etc . . . , The meal ended and Juane' offered to bring Kya home. On the way Juane' explained that most of the rich truckers, doctors and business men/women that comes through the bank are doing banking business but they are also the clientele that makes it possible to maintain her house, car note and food on the table for her family.

Juane' said "as far as I know there was no sex involved, at least on my end but I can't speak for the other ladies. The good thing about it is that you would only work the weekends with an occasional weekday or holiday. She also asked Kya to think about it, and mentioned that maybe she could do it for a little while and if she didn't like she could walk away and still keep her job.

Even as Juane parked the car in front of Kya's apartment, Kya was still sporting a goofy grin of awe! She didn't even remember if she thanked Juane for the ride. She walked the path to the buildings front door in zombie like state while still exchanging pleasantries with her neighbors. Could she do it? Is the money worth the illegal activity? Kya had a lot to think about!!!

The Try Out

———

After that very strange and enlighten meeting Kya went inside and headed to her favorite spot in the apartment to think, the outside balcony. She started weighing the pros and cons of why to do it. It would mean a move to a larger apartment, a new car, and just plain be able to catch up on bills and live normally (without having to rob Peter to pay Paul). She stood up and leaned over the banister, watching her neighbors drag home from their penny ante jobs while toting a bag for either the makings of tonight's supper or a bottle or two of spirits to ease the pain of the day.

There was Ms. Poers a seventy-nine year old grandmother-mother of three. Her daughter Kathy got strung out on crack cocaine and died, a year ago of AIDS, leaving her to raise children all over again. Their ages ranged from eleven to fifteen. Even before Kathy's passing Ms. Poers and Kya would sit out on the patio where Ms. Poers often talked about how she struggles and Kya was more than sure raising preteens couldn't make things any easier on the sweet old lady.

Then there was Jackson who was sitting out in his usual spot on the stoop, shaking mostly from withdrawal and not the so call music he says plays in his head. His habit whatever it was had him hunting for new jobs every other week. Often Jackson would put on a dancing show; he would spread out a cardboard box and relive his pop locking bugaloo days. It was quite entertaining on his good day but when the grapes had a hold of him it was just plain comical to see.

Lastly in the four-plex was Babette. Other than her playing loud music Kya liked Babette a lot. Babette kept Kya abreast of the latest styles, dances and sayings, she was like the little sister Kya never had. Sometimes Kya would babysit Babette's youngest—twin girls; Shayla and Shanna. These two three year old cherubs called Kya auntie Ya Ya and came over every time to help Kya make homemade chocolate chip cookies. Babette didn't work but she had several different gentlemen in out of her apartment. Kya was pretty sure Babette was prostituting but as long as she didn't endanger her five children it wasn't any of her business. All Kya knew was she didn't want to end up like either of her neighbors.

Kya woke up on Sunday morning with her mind already made up. She dressed and left for church early so she could at least sit on one of the front pews, that way she wouldn't have to battle Sister Mayfield and her many big, huge and colorful, flowered, thing-a-ma-jig of a hat. Because Kya was a firm believer that "the eyes are the window to the soul" maybe the pastor could read what she intended to do and somehow preach a sermon worthy of her changing her mind! Even if that didn't happen she wanted to talk with God, in hopes of his understanding and forgiveness. She stayed for the second service, grabbed a plate of the Salisbury steak dinner that was offered afterwards and walked the five blocks home with a plan in mind.

On Monday dressed and waiting outside for Juane', Kya played over and over in her mind what her role would be in the somewhat felonious act. She was going to play it cool and just ease her way into it. Once she arrived at work she approached Mr. Barrow and gave him her terms and conditions of participation. First he eyed her as if she was crazy and then he told Kya to come back during her lunch and he could fill her in some more on how things worked.

Normally Kya would take her hour for lunch to get away from the hustle of the bank, but today Kya decided to eat in the break room first to ease the nerves jumping around in her stomach and secondly to make sure she had enough time to have that talk with Mr. Barrow. She put her things in the garbage and straightens out her dress, walked thru the lobby and knocked Mr. Barrow's door.

He was on the phone and motion for her to have a seat. From what she could tell from his end of the conversation was that a new client was coming aboard and he was writing something in what looks like a ledger.

Once seated he put in front of her a listing of names, dates and times. Mr. Barrow said he only had time to explain the gist of the organization: each teller had three clients, two male and one female. You meet for cocktails at a designated bar to see if your compatible. Then they come in to see me for specific details, like what is expected, payment, and an itinerary of each social gathering we are needed for. I make sure everyone look up to par by making sure manicure, pedicure, hair and wardrobe is scheduled to be done.

Our clients can be married or single. Most of them are away from home and their spouses are too busy to join them. The men are mostly lonely or too embarrassed to show up to prestige events alone and the women, in the closet lesbians that just wants the company of a beautiful lady to have dinner, movie or attend a play with. As I said I explain to the clientele there is absolutely no sex expected and contracts are sign to seal the deal.

Your first meeting is this Friday with a man name Jacob McFarland. He is expecting you for drinks and MJ's on Portland Avenue at eight. So I've set up your initial medi, pedi and hair appointment for you on Wednesday. Get with Nykole for the detail and stipend for clothing. Oh yeah if you ever want to see the details of the account look up Merry Ladies and I have every receipt here to account for every penny. Kya we just provide companionship nothing more and nothing less. Just relax, make money and have fun.

Monday thru Thursday went by pretty quickly. Kya got her nails and feet taken care of on Wednesday and Thursday went shopping for clothes in addition to purchasing something she always wanted but couldn't afford; a full lace human hair wig. She couldn't believe she was going to go thru with it but after arriving home and retrieving several overdue bills out of the mailbox; her mind was made up. Friday morning found Kya nauseas with her stomach tied in knots tighter than a sailor's rope in a four hitch. She called in sick but reassured Mr. Barrow that she would be at MJ's that night, on time and looking stunting.

Kya slept until four o'clock and awoke to walk on her treadmill for an hour, plus to eat light salad for an early dinner. She had to psyche herself up for tonight's event so she put on her Mel Waiters "Woman In Need" cd to play her favorite track, "Got My Whiskey." Buck naked, she started humming and dancing along with the song, tweaked her eyebrows just a little, put Nair (hair removal lotion) in the areas of her underarm, pubic area and legs as she gather her lacey under wear and clothing. Its six o'clock so Kya poured herself a glass of crown royal squeezed a little lemon juice in it then head to the shower and dress for tonight.

Kya arrived fifteen minutes early so she could gather her bearings before Mr. McFarland showed. When the waiter arrived she order another crown royal being careful not to mix her liquor and risk throwing up. Mr. McFarland showed up at exactly eight. He was six feet, athletically built, smelling of expensive cologne along with a pair of stiffly starched blue jeans, light blue pullover shirt and matching blue jean jacket, handsome and white.

It never accrued to her that he would be white, with quick thinking Kya eased away to the restroom to take another look at her appearance. She walked into the ladies restroom and proceeded straight to the mirror. There she stood looking at her reflection in admiration as she took in all of her five feet five inch dark chocolate frame, oval shaped face, slightly squinty eyes with deep craters for dimples. The dress she chose to wear was deep red with a v-cut that exposed enough cleavage to turn a man's head but not so much to be considered a slut. Then she turned to look at what was considered to her cupid's arrow, her bountiful bootie. Things seem to be in place so she turned took one more look at her makeup and adjusted her wig, took a deep breath and headed back to the table hoping that Mr. McFarland had been seated already.

As she approached the table Mr. McFarland stood with an outstretched hand to greet her. His piercing blue eyes seemed to look right through her and she had to blink to keep her nerves. Electricity struck as soon as their hands touch in a handshaking union, the smirk on his face told Kya that he felt it too as he gestured for her to have a seat. He introduced himself as Jacob the horny toad, then laughed a deep hearty laugh. Kya cringed a little at the vision of fighting arms and hands off her body but placed herself in the heavy padded chair anyway.

"Well hello horny toad, my name is Kya how do you do?" she said and they both laugh loudly as on lookers wonder what was so funny. Jacob said he use that line as an ice breaker to see what type of sense of humor a person has. From then on the date went well. They talked about sports; he was a Cowboy and Laker fan. The two teams Kya despised the most and she exclaimed she was a Saints fan but didn't follow basketball enough to have a favorite team. From there they discussed favorite food, TV shows, holidays and drinks. Kya was feeling comfortable because of his demeanor or the three crown royal on the rocks she drank; either way she was having a good time.

By the time the conversation turned to family the manager was at the table letting them know that they would be closing in thirty minutes. "Wow, Jacob said. Young lady I have had such a good time sitting her just talking and staring into your big beautiful eyes with those cute dimples that play pee-a-boo in your face, that I lost track of time." Kya the next time I am in Little Pebbles can I see you again? She replied with a sure Jacob I really enjoyed myself and I would like that very much. Jacob then stood up, walked over to pull her chair back, helped her put on her silk wrap, they chatted some more as they walked arm in arm toward the exit door of Wally's and her awaiting taxi.

Kya paid the cab, hopped over Jackson with his shrine of liquor bottles and mumbles of words, to the elevator and her favorite spot in her apartment, the patio. She plugged in her Scentsy fragrant warmer, loaded it with her favorite scent of blueberry cheesecake, grabbed a bottle of wine and sat there going over the date in her head. Made an entry in her new journal she bought to keep track of her dating stories. Once she was finish writing she notice it was after two a.m. She decided to showered then journey off to bed to rest up for her next date later on that day.

On Saturday Kya awoke to the fighting sounds of Babette and one of her latest overnight guest arguing over money with her children yelling in the background. She couldn't decide whether to get up and see if help was needed or let it play itself out, given what happen last time. It was a week before Christmas and she was guessing Babette had a gentlemen caller with all the moaning and head board banging noises she heard. It turns out her beau at the time didn't take the news of their breakup to well and was holding her hostage.

The moans were Babette trying to speak thru the handkerchief in her mouth and the banging was the resistance of her not wanting to be tied up. Kya heard babies twin crying for almost three hours and decided to call the police, the cops found Babette and took the guy into custody. The day after he got out of jail they were back together and she dropped the charges citing that they were playing sex games. So Kya was not getting involved, put the pillow over her head and went back to sleep; after all a girl needs her beauty rest for her second date on her second job sort of speak.

The alarm started beeping at noon, Kya hit the snooze button a couple of times before finally getting up to do her work out routine. Next on the agenda was to run errands, shop for a new dress for tonight's festivities then go home to yet again physic herself up to do something that was somewhat illegal. She kept thinking of the money and laid across her bed to glance at the apartment hunter's magazine, she picked up while shopping, to the pages of the apartments and houses in a better part of town where she longed to live.

Living better! That thought alone made her mojo flow and she laid out her dress, showered, grabbed her self a bud light lime, plugged in her scentsy, this time opting for the coconut lemongrass fragrance, and started doing calculations about the money she should be receiving. After being satisfied of her profit portion she did her prep routine only this time she chose "just got paid" by Johnny Kemp well aware it wasn't Friday night but somehow the song fit.

Kya decided to wear her pale blue one shoulder dress that angled on the opposite side at the legs. She donned a pair of skin tone pantyhose but decide to opt out on underwear because she didn't want a panty line, she took care in applying her make-up, spritz and brushed her secure lace wig into place, grabbed a pair of penny size imitation opal diamond studs, sprayed a few shots of perfume on both sides of her neck as she slide into her opal and blue shoes. She took a final glance in the full length bathroom mirror, threw a kiss at her beautiful image and grabbed her purse on the way out of the door.

Tonight's meeting place was Brino's Bar and Grill. Her date was to meet her at six for cocktails and dinner. Her name was Laverna Duvernay, some rich heir's daughter and the owner of several successful restaurants. Now Kya thoughts were she would be this butch looking woman with a short crop cut and dressed as a man but she was surprised. Laverna was stunning!

This made her even more nervous than her date with McFarland. If Laverna had been masculine looking she could at least in her mind image her as a man, but this sister was a golden caramel colored with what looks like a pair of double D's hanging out of her cream and teal blouse that match her teal pants and shoes. She sauntered over to the table in what seem like an effortless walk on six inch stilettos. She had to be at least five feet six or five seven with just as much ass as Kya did. In other words she is what today's generation of men calls a dime piece.

Laverna had every male head turning as she mesmerized them with her scent of expensive perfume. Once she reached the table she jokingly said "Man! It's just like the cartoons, as if I have an invisible finger leading them by the nose." Kya nodded her head in agreement and began to relax. They ordered shrimp cocktails and quickly started talking like they were old friends. Laverna voice was soothing. Kya forgot she was supposed to be on a date up until after the entrees; Laverna reached across the table to hold her hand.

Kya pulled away and continue to rapidly chat about the first thing that came to her mind. Laverna sensed she was nerves, leaned back in the booth and cracked a wicked smile. She studied Kya face for moment while she sipped on her drink. I guess it is time for us to part my dear; I've taken up enough of your time. Hopefully we can see each other again. With that being said Laverna stood up, paid the check and left with the same air of attention she waltzed in with.

After Laverna drove off Kya had the host hail her cab and rode home in silence. She was too embarrassed to call a cab in Laverna presence. This woman is special Kya was thinking to herself, I can't wait to jot this down. Once at her apartment she went straight to her notebook to write about her date. She summed up the whole experience of her weekend and then in a separate notebook her calculations of the weekend to present to Mr. Barrows on Monday morning. Now it bed time, church first thing in the morning.

Trouble Rears Its Head

On Monday, Kya woke up two hours early because Juane had phoned Sunday night, just before she dozed off to sleep, to inform her she wouldn't be coming in to work so that meant catching two buses and a six block walk to the bank. She always believed in getting to work at least fifteen minutes early to prepare and therefore at the designated time ready to work. Kya whole focus while riding the LPT (Little Pebble Transit) was looking at every car for a general ideal on which car to buy.

Once off the bus, Kya started her walk toward the bank. As she made her way to the branch she notice a car with tinted windows make a circle around the bank, then park into the first spot on the lot. As far as she knew no one she worked with owned a candy red Ford Escape, so she kept walking past and toward the open Walgreens store across the traffic lanes on the corner. Not wanting to be a hostage of some sort, she stood left of the door entrance so she could get a good view of the bank.

Just then Mr. Barrows pulled into the lot right next to the unknown car and rolled down his windows while the driver of the other car did the same. It seem like words were exchanged by the way Mr. Barrows head was bobbing. Then an arm stretched out with a manila colored envelope, Mr. Barrows took the envelope and the car pulled away.

As she approached Mr. Barrows's car he was rifling through the envelope and once he saw Kya he quickly tossed it in his briefcase and got out of the car. Oh Ms. Martinley I didn't see you, how was your weekend? Kya replied it was great and on the interesting side. He then shifted his briefcase as if he was adjusting its contents and walked toward the bank door with a questionable look on his face.

It was a typical busy Monday; everyone who didn't make it to the bank on Friday was there and then some. Mr. Barrows came to make the usual deposit for the Merry Ladies account. He made the announcement that all was good and that the clients had nothing but good things to say about the new comer. Mr. Barrows turned to Kya and said "Keep up the good work Kya before long you too can have all the things you long for and some of the things you just plain want!"

Dominicki clapped in unison with Barbara while saying how happy they were that Kya was a perfect fit; then Juane', Dominicki and Barbara started chanting mo money! Mo money! Mo money! Everyone was glad that things were going well and even though she cheered Nykole's facial expression and body language said something very different. Kya guessed she wasn't the only one caught that because Mr. Barrows called Nykole into his office and when she return she was mumbling something about her being the head bitch behind the line and everywhere else and vowed she wasn't going to let no one mess things up; marched to her office and slammed the door close.

By the time Kya returned from her lunch, everyone had gotten their stipend and date assignment for weekend. Two dates, free dinner, wine and dancing, new clothes and pampering session and still cleared thousand per week was an ideal job as far as Kya as concern. She intended to ride out the wave as longs as her morals would let her. On her way to the bus stop Kya was doing some calculation and figured between her paycheck and the side job she could make her ends meet but the only questions was what to do first, buy a car or move to a new apartment?

She didn't linger over that question long because when she arrived home her front door was wide open. A policeman was standing among a mess in her living room. He introduced himself as Officer Midway and told her that a neighbor heard lots of noise, she knew you were at work and called us. He said they had a look around and no one was there, but she may want to see if anything was missing.

After all the chaos was over, Kya grabbed the newspaper to seek a new apartment. She was glad nothing was taken just things broken and strewed about and doubly glad she didn't have her new earned money in her apartment for someone to take. She couldn't help but laugh out loud at herself because as soon as she saw the police she thought they were there to arrest her for her somewhat illegal activity this past weekend. Then she had a stern talk with herself to not to be so paranoid and made a promise to start a bank account as soon as she get to work in the morning.

Tuesday she started her new account with Bank of Deposit N.A., Wednesday came in and went with haste. Now its Thursday, it was to be the second meeting she will be attending and she still was as nervous as if it was her first. Everyone arrived on time, ordered drinks and Mr. Barrows talked straight business and gave everyone their money envelope as they all ate. He also informed everyone that this weekend rotation was going to be different with Nykole, Barbara, Dominicki and Juane continuing with their rotation but Kya was going to have the same clients. Kya could tell that didn't sit well with the other especially Nykole but no argument was had and they ended the evening.

On the ride home Juane said you sure must've made an impression because we've never veered away from the plan. We have all tried to bring it up in our meetings but Mr. Barrows wouldn't hear of it. I don't think Nykole is too happy with you, did you see those glaring eyes? I wanted to laugh but I think she probably would have hit me. I personally don't care because as long as I get my money to help me maintain my life style I'm good. Nykole thinks too high of herself anyway so it is about time someone takes her down a peg. Word to the wise my friend, watch your back, and please be careful was the last thing Juane said to Kya as she was getting out of the car. Kya made inside, turned on her music and opened her envelop. There was at least one thousand more than last week. She would have to ask Mr. Barrows about that the next day at work.

Now Friday's were always the second worst days, it was full of long lines of customers looking to get in, cash their checks or make a deposit and get out. By this time Kya had developed a rapport with her regulars and looking to develop the same with the new ones. For some reason today was not going that great. Nykole seems to pick apart everything Kya said or did; she chastised her for asking a customer about their plans for their anniversary; she monitored her phone calls telling Kya that this was a place of business when she received a call from a potential landlord and throughout the day made snide remarks about people trying to take over but she was having it.

Just as Kya decided to speak up Mr. Barrows walked in to make a deposit, so she changed her mind but opting to speak with him in his office later. Kya was available to make his deposit but he waited on Juane' to finish with her customer and instructed her to only make the deposit. On his way back to his office Kya decided to walk with him, she asked Mr. Barrow about the extra thousand in her envelop and he response was that her clients really enjoyed their date and paid and extra five hundred dollars apiece for the next date with her. He reminded Kya that he was making an exception and no sex was to be involved or she was out.

It was Barbara's Friday to get off early so Kya had to pick her time to speak with Mr. Barrows about Nykole's behavior; again she opted to do so during her early lunch. She quickly gobbled up her Taco Bell nacho bell grande and slurped her Pepsi spilling some on her uniform, but she didn't care she needed to speak with her supervisor before the day was done.

Mr. Barrows wasn't too thrilled about her interruption but told her to take a seat anyway. He listened intensely and a said he will look into the matter but not to worry some people fear competition and you my dear are her competition. Just keep up the good work at this branch and with the Merry Ladies and you will be okay. With that he patted Kya on the shoulder and sent her out the door. She felt duped and decided to take matters into her on hands.

It was finally time to leave work. The ride home with Juane was very informative; she gave Kya the 411 on Nykole. It seems she had been working with the bank for a long time and the top lady of choice when it came to the Merry Ladies. Juane also said she figures Nykole probably feels threaten because until you came along she was the only one to get special requests. Girl if I was you I wouldn't worry about it, besides Mr. Barrows seems to have your back. So go with the flow, have fun, spend your money wisely and oh yeah save because you never know when all this will come to an end. Now I got to go and get ready for my date, but first find a sitter because my regular is graduating from beauty school tonight.

Babette was waiting on the door step, she seem to have been crying. The child protection services had come to take her kids away. One of the neighbors or even her own parents had reported her leaving her kids in the home alone. She went on talking through sniffles saying how she was a good parent and rarely left her kids alone. She did everything she could to make ends meet. Yes, I do my little whoring on the side but my kid doesn't want for anything. They have food, the latest clothes, video games and a momma that loves them very much. She asked Kya if she could be a character witness once she had to go before the judge. Kya felt for Babette and assured her she would do everything she could to help, then walked Babette to her apartment with a hug at the door before heading to hers to prepare for Mr. McFarland.

Round two with Jacob and Laverna

⌒

Tonight's meeting place was a karaoke country bar. In her usual pep routine she put on some music, only this time she was listening to Carrie Underwood's "Before He Cheats" Reba's "If I Was a Boy" followed by Keith Urban and a few other country artist. She didn't get the same revved up vibe as if she was listening to r&b or blues but she was trying to get into the country mood. She put a pair of dark black denim jeans with the matching jacket with a red halter top underneath. Top offed with a black cowgirl hat over her ponytail and red and black snake skins boots. She decided on not bring a purse so she placed her license and five twenties in her pocket.

Honky Tonky Karaoke Country Bar was just that. Complete with mechanical bull riding, hay on the floor and a sea of denim of all colors with the smells of hot leather and barbeque. They choose a corner booth that had a bird eye view of the dance floor. As soon as they were seated the waitress came to take their orders, bud light and a bud lime for the lady Jacob said. Kya notice Jacobs was tapping his foot to music and seemed anxious to dance. She wasn't about to make a fool of herself, she tired the line dancing thing before and couldn't get the swing of it.

Two buckets of beer later, Kya found herself dancing on the floor with Jacob. They were twirling and line dancing just having a real good time. Then the people started rootin tootin scooting and it was time for both of them to get off the dance floor. That dance was over both their heads. By this time Kya had enough of the partiers trying to ride the mechanical bull Rex with failure, so she blew the horn that informed people that there was a new first timer on the ride.

She hopped on using the stirrups, threw her jacket over to McFarland, gave the command to start the bull. A slow downward motion, then upward, downward, upward, downward upward, then it went a little faster. She was holding up good. Then with a quick jerk the bull with crazy, those upward downward motions began to come with bucking. Grabbing on tighter and entering her two minute mark Kya was thinking it was just like have sex and she could do that with her eyes close.

Three second later Kya found herself head first into a bushel of hay, she was embarrassed but the crowd gave her hoots, cheers and thunderous clapping. The emcee announced that she broke the new comer's record by two seconds and her name was going on their greenhorn wall of fame. She took off her cowgirl hat and raised it in a victorious wave, but the walk back over to the booth was something rather difficult.

Jacob senses her pain and came over to help her back to her seat. He said, Kya just as I thought you're my type of gal but it's time to get you home, you're going to be pretty sore in the morning young lady. Now let me walk you to your car. Kya was hesitant to tell Mr. McFarland that her car was still sitting at the bank parking lot and she didn't have time to rent car; so she lied and said it was in the shop, but she would be happy if he would call a cab for her.

Heck no Kya, I will give you a ride home in my limo. Jacob helped her into her jacket, placed her hat on his head, his on her and two stepped all the way to his limo. Once inside he put in a couple of cd, Kya braced herself to hear more country music but instead "Moments of love" by the Art of Noise sneaked through the speakers.

This was her favorite song; he was honestly listening last week on their date. Keeping in mind she drank two buckets of beer, in each bucket was six bottles and this was her fantasy song to make mad passionate love to, Kya slid closer to the window for some air.

She felt like she was on fire and he seem oblivious to her state and keep right on chatting about their night.

By the time they arrived at her apartment, Kya was horny as hell. Not wanting the date to end, so he played more of her favorite artist, Gerald Levert, Floetry, and Jill Scott as they talked at least another hour. Kya started to yarn and Jacob took that as a cue that it was her bed time. Jacob motion for the driver to stay in the limo, got out to open her door, walked her to the door step and gave her a mind numbing kiss. Place her hat on her head and said see you next week.

Too sexually wound up to sleep or write about her night, Kya reached way back in her nightstand where her battery operated friend Sting was hiding and brought him to life. It had been two years since she was in a relationship and one year since she had sex, so her mission tonight was relief. Bzzzzzzzzzzzz! Sing to me Sting!

Saturday morning Kya woke up with Sting lying beside her knee and dribble of spittle coming from her mouth. Damn! Sting must've given her a good work over because she was sore as hell plus hung over. Then she remembered the mechanical bull, threw herself back on the bed and laughed hysterically.

Once her laughing fit was over Kya check on the condition of Sting, he was dead. Oh well she said, I need to put batteries on the shopping list. Exercise, light breakfast and errand time which consist of bill pay, grocery shopping and off for a medi/pedi because tonight it was Laverna date night. While she didn't have the means to be porcelain ready like her. She still had to maintain to keep the clients' interests.

Tonight's attire is a silver, cris cross backing with spaghetti strap dress. The main reason she bought the dress was because of the long slit that ran up and down the side of her leg. She remember grandmamma Lou always saying whenever you buy a skirt or dress always make it has a split that shows off your legs. Well this was a little more than a split but who cares.

Kya made sure her full lace wig was still attached securely and then put it in a beautiful up swept bun. With makeup already applied she grazed through her jewelry chest to give her assemble some color. She picked out a pair of multi-colored earrings with matching bracelet; it had the same color silver in it. She sprayed the new cologne she purchased on a whim, the name of the fragrance is Coach Poppy and it blended well with her body chemistry.

Also during her errand run Kya decided to rent a rental car, she would have to remember that she drove to the restaurant and limit herself to two or three drinks. On her way to the car she ran into Babette, she was talking with a group of women. They were laughing so Kya was guessing things were going ok with Babette and her family because she smiled and wave at Kya as she was driving away in her rental.

Laverna beat Kya there. She was sitting down and blindly commanding attention. The waiters were yet again falling all over themselves to serve her. Once she spotted Kya she leaned forward to whisper something into Eric's ear, the waiter we had last weekend. He smiled, looked back at Kya and walked away. He reappeared with a bottle of champagne and two menus. Laverna was stunningly dressed again. They were almost mirror image with the exception that Laverna was wearing real pearl accessories. Great minds think alike she said as Kya took a seat.

Laverna ask "What would you like to eat today my lovely lady friend?" That made Kya squirm in her seat a little which in turn made Laverna serious. She poured herself and Kya a glass of champagne, chuckled to herself, took a deep breath and said we need to seriously talk, then slid closer to Kya.

Look Kya I'm a married woman, I would say happily but obviously I am not or neither one of us would be here. My family frowns upon lesbian and I'm wouldn't call myself that anyway. Let's just say I am very, very curious. I want to feel the pleasures of woman, who knows a woman body and sexual responses better than a woman.

I've met with Juane', Barbara, Dominicki and Nykole and they are lovely women but not what I am looking for. I'm looking for someone thick, confident, sensitive, spiritual, speak with your eyes and body and most important can keep a secret. Like I said those other women doesn't seem if they can hold water on their tongue.

I have money, two sons and a daughter, a husband that ironically I do love; all the fake friends' money can buy but no true soul. What I mean by that is I work hard, sometimes making decisions that I don't like but it is part of my life style. Also, I play hard going to parties, red carpet events and stuff like that but in the end there is no one there that feels me deeply.

You would be very well taken care of and all I ask is for one day out of the month to get together and let our hair down. Then Laverna reached in to her stunning platinum bag and handed Kya an envelope. She said don't open it until you get home. Now let's order a delicious meal then go dance the night away.

They ended up a Clinger D's a popular night club in Little Pebble. Kya thought Laverna was a great dancer, she hung in there with the youngster popping it to Jeremiah and 50 cent song "put it down on me, "hand-danced to Mel Waiters "two steps." Also Laverna and Kya did the bus stop, cha-cha and electric slide and a host of other dances until three in morning.

As they were walking to the car, Laverna stopped short, grabbed Kya, slid down her spaghetti strap and began to fondle her breast. A sigh of shock and pleasure escaped Kya mouth when Laverna leaned down and begin to suck them. When Kya didn't resist Laverna lean her on the hood of her own Mercedes Benz, using her teeth she open the slit on Kya dressed and began to lick her secret spot. After five minutes of darting and teasing she stood up, looked Kya in the eye and said there is more to come. Think about what I said, no one has to know. Good night my dear and she drove away leaving Kya confused as she walked back to her rental car.

By the time she made it back to her apartment Kya became ashamed of her behavior in the parking lot. She could've stopped Laverna or a least put some kind of resistance but hell it felt so good. She really needed to get herself a steady man which is what she vowed as turned on the lamp in the living room. This was definitely a journal night so after a hot shower Kya grabbed her composition notebook and wrote with a quick vengeances because she a yet another date with Sting.

Sunday morning Kya decided not to go to church, but stay at home and seriously weighed her life's plan. She listed the pros and cons of what and why she was doing the Merry Ladies. The goals were to make enough money to live better, buy a new car, and make enough to attend college and get her bachelor's degree. Now she found that she has options, three of them in fact. Option one, be more that a date with Jacob McFarland the millionaire; option two, be a once a month lesbian to the heir's daughter Laverna Duvernay and option three walk away from it all and go back to Ponde, Louisiana.

After writing she closed her composition and spent the rest of day lounging around and setting up appointments to see apartments for the week to come. Although she didn't go to church Kya still remembered to read her bible lesson for that day; then settle down to call her mom before tuning in for the night. In her prayer she asked God for forgiveness for what she was planning to do and with that she went to sleep.

The Plan of a Lottery

At the bank there were daily operational bank huddles; one in the morning before opening and the second meeting was held if time aloud during the evening hours before closing. On this particular Monday the daily morning meeting consisted of more than just banking business. Mr. Barrows had a late evening managers meeting so he was leaving at two which was an hour before our daily evening meeting would have originally scheduled. He started off with our customer service poll, he said we were still number one in our region; our checking, savings and loans goals are being met with a consistency and we reach our branching quota and will receive that extra payout.

Next Mr. Barrows said on to Merry Ladies business, since there have been some complaints about not following the rules of alternating our dates; we are going to have a lottery. I need you all to write a short sentence about your last week dates. On our Thursday meeting we will put the names in a pouch and whomever you pick that will be your standing client from here on out. Then last and least Mr. Barrows gave out the weekly stipends that they were all waiting for.

At seven Kya was to meet with Jerry Murphy the manager of her potential new apartment on the North side of town. She was schedule to get off at six and it would quite a drive to that side of town due to heavy traffic. The problem was she had mention her dilemma to Mr. Barrow and he said he would be leaving early and that Nykole would be in charge in his absence, providing she didn't had an emergency whatever Nykole decides goes. Kya was just going to have to suck in wind and ask Nykole if she can leave at least thirty minutes before her time to get off. The thing is at the point Nykole seem to be against her lately. If it wasn't about Kya's clothes or lunchtime, it was this or her that; Kya was wondering how much longer she could hang in there without a confrontation.

Just then Nykole called Kya into her office. She said "I had just gotten off the phone with Mr. Barrow and your request to leave early was denied stating I need you Kya to stay your entire schedule time because Barbara leaves early." Then Nykole said "Kya what I'm, about to say is off the record. First of all I want you to know I am not vain. I work out and buy the finer things so I can be the head B I T C H! It seems everyone knows the rules except you my dear and that needs to changer or you will be sorry."

"Secondly, Nykole rumbled, on Thursday during the lottery I need you to put back the following people if you pull their names: Laverna Duvernay, Jacob McFarland and Darrius Stomp. They are the most lucrative and very important to the Merry Ladies success and I don't think you have what it takes to handle such an import task." Kya looked at Nykole and ask "is my job with the bank in jeopardy if I don't?" Nykole just snorted a no now get the hell out of my office; slamming the door behind Kya. The rest of the day was so tense you could have use a very sharp machete and still couldn't get through all the tension. It turned out to be very long day.

This Thursday Wally's was unusually busy, but Merry Ladies table was still available for them because the manager and hostess Susan, who owned and worked at Wally's for the past thirteen years, had reserved their table on a weekly basis for the past three years along with remembering their drink of choice. The table wasn't in the corner but just tucked away enough for privacy that things could be discussed without the worry of someone ear hustling. For Susan troubles she got a very handsome tip so she was always glad when Thursday came around.

Of course we had to wait for Nykole and her eight ten bravado to start the meeting but it didn't stop any one from ordering their drinks and Kya led off with a tall long island tea. She had never had one before but Juane swears that they are so good. She did warn Kya that it was a sneak-up on you type of drink so gulping is something Kya shouldn't do.

Eight thirty, no Nykole and Mr. Barrow was becoming more furious at each passing minute. He was strict about holding the meeting for at least an hour so every concern, gripe, or potential new client could be voiced then we all could have a meal together then go home. Mr. Barrow often said that since we are at work just as much as we are home that we are family and we should break bread together at least once a week

Nine o'clock again no Nykole, so we all decided to start the meeting while everyone ate their meal. Mr. Barrow decided to hold off on the lottery until next meeting because Nykole wasn't there. He again reiterated the reason for the lottery. Gave everyone their envelope and like a Papa bear hugged us all and said to be careful on our Merry Lady journey.

Friday morning didn't start out well at all. Kya missed her first bus, decided to walk on over to her second bus route and just as she turned the bend the second bus was pulling away from the curb. She cursed Juane daughter for being sick and then quickly ask God for forgiveness for thinking bad about the situation. So she plopped down on the bench to wait for the next bus.

Suddenly a champagne blue Aston Martin pulled up to the light. The window rolled down and Nykole head appeared. She called Kya over to the car, asked about last night meeting and when the light turned green peeled off nearly rolling over her foot. Kya thought that was just plain mean, but it is Nykole's car and she didn't have to offer a ride even if they were going to the same place. Kya screamed after Nykole that she would get a bigger, better, stronger and faster car than hers. She burst into laughter as she walked back to the bus stop bench for quoting the Six Million Dollar Woman opening. Once she recovered from her outburst she made a serious inner note to do just that, and then hopped on the just arrived bus to work.

Of course Kya was twenty minutes late and Nykole was waiting at the door with a write up. She handed it to Kya with a grin on her face and walked into her office. Kya made a mental note to herself, turned to Barbara who was standing next to her reading the write-up and said I see this is going to be a battle but I'm up to the challenge. Kya signed the paper, marches into Nykole's office, placed it on her desk smiled her prettiest smile and headed back to her station to work.

Mr. Barrow had arrived at work as Kya was leaving out and headed to Nykole's office, shutting the door and there were a lot of muddle talking. From what they could hear he told Nykole that if thing were going to operate smoothly he needed cooperation and that she was not above being replaced. As he trotted through the door he reminded her that if she wanted a certain thing to remain a secret she had better not miss any more meetings.

All day Kya tried to concentrate on her job but those parting words that Mr. Barrows spoke to Nykole played over and over in her head. Those words intrigued Kya to the point that she had to find out what the secret was. Her plans were to stop at nothing to find out. Kya was so consumed with the secret that she was out of balanced at the end of the day and in looking for her error she discovered she had deposited a check as cash, given a check back to the customer after she had cashed it. So she reversed the transaction so it read a check deposit and had to call Mrs. Barnes to see if she had given her the check back.

Mrs. Barnes looked inside her purse with the money envelope and discovered that Kya did indeed give her the check back and promise to bring it to the bank first thing in the morning. Kya thanked her and apologized to her for her inconvenience of having to come back to the bank. Then she and Juane' closed the bank for the weekend by setting the alarm and locking the door.

Kya took the ride home with Juane to find out some more dirt on Nykole. Come on Juane, there has got to be more to Nykole than being top lady with Merry Ladies said Kya. What's her status, family or something because she can't only live for the bank?

Alright Kya, I will tell what the rumor mill is on her. Rumor has it that she wasn't always the queen bee. She lied, schemed, stole and booted out the other assistant manager. She started as a teller, worked her way up, got her shot with Merry Ladies and will stop at nothing to stay on top, so again my best advice to you is to heed her warnings and try to stay on her good side.

Nykole all but said that during the proposed lottery that if I got certain clients to put them back because she wanted them. It was weird as if my job depended on it and to me it seems impossible considering what we are doing is a little illegal. Besides I'm only in it to make enough money to buy a car and a better place to live so Nykole can stay the queen as far as I am concern.

That's good to hear, Juane said because I really think she is an evil person, don't mess with her Kya. It's for your own good. Wow Juane', Kya said. You act like she is part of the mafia or something, it's not that serious. Well thanks for the ride home once again. I promise a few more weeks and you will be rid of me as your shotgun buddy.

You just have fun on your journey tonight, hey who's on your circuit anyway Juane asked? We haven't had the lottery yet so it is Mr. McFarland and tonight he is preparing dinner for me on his yacht or something. I got an email saying to dress elegantly and bring a bathing suit. I can't swim but I sure enjoy eating.

Still leaning out of the window Juane said you got it easy at least you don't have a fat slob want to be rapper, with too much jewelry, bad breathe and sweats when he eats. I mean it's like rain pouring down and I don't mean money. It happens whether the food is spicy or not, I believe maybe it's because he is just too fat. I literally have to wear a rain coat or put up my umbrella to stay dry. Girl, you are crazy Juane. Maybe you should just wear pleather so the sweat would just roll off of you. Well see you on Monday and stay dry Kya said as she closed the car door and walked away laughing at her co-worker that seems to be coming a good friend.

The Issue of Tissue

⁓

Now it's time to pump myself up for the date Kya was thinking as she pour herself her favorite drink of crown royal and water with a twist of lemon. She took a big gulp and headed straight for the CD player. Hmm! Motivation by Kelly Rowlands will do just nicely for tonight's escapade.

Dressed in a green and canary yellow shift dress, with a yellow bikini underneath, Kya pick up the phone to call Jacob as instructed in the email so she can be picked when she was ready. Jacob answered the phone on the first ring and told Kya to prepare to be amazed and the car will be there in thirty minutes so Kya took that time to start her entry into her dairy. She lowered the volume on the CD player and wrote simply "changes to come" closed her book and looked over the apartment renter book of high rise apartments that she hopefully will be living in soon. As she was narrowing down her choices there was a knock at the door. One more squirt of perfume and once over in the mirror Kya open the door; there stood the driver with a bouquet of roses six count each of pink, yellow, red and white.

After giving Kya the flowers the driver bowed then led the way to the limousine. Inside the limo, there Jacob supplied champagne, more roses, her favorite music and a black velvet box. Kya eyes bucked wide open as she open up the box from Adele's a very expensive jewelry store and there on a blue silk strip was a slim emerald anklet. Kya lifted her leg and gently put on the beautiful anklet that brought out the green color in her shift dress then sat back and enjoyed the music as they rode to the marina.

The Frenchmen street wharf was beautiful. There were at least five yachts docked there and Jacob's yacht stood out among them. A great big Stetson Flag hung at the masses and Kya could hear the cd he made just for her playing in the back ground. As she approached, Jacob was standing there handsomely tan as ever with a Bellini in one hand, well dressed and orchards in hand. Also nestle all around the cabin were candles with white, orange and yellow Lillie; Kya all-time favorite flowers.

Kya melted like butter as she stepped onto the yacht and saw all the food spread out on the table. Lobster, gnocchi, caviar, fruits, prime ribs and countless of other delectable. It was so much food; she didn't know where to start. When Kya eyed those white and milk chocolate covered strawberries she nearly dove in head first but Jacob grabbed her hands and lead her to the table.

Hold on little lady can I at least get a hello first? Kya was embarrassed beyond belief now, she apologize to Jacob for acting like a starving monkey but where she was from that was considered hitting the jackpot of food. Then she slowly lifted her dress just enough to reveal the anklet and his Cheshire grin told her he approved. He pulled the chair out for them both and the dining began.

They talked and ate some much that Kya hadn't realized the yacht moved until they made their way up to rear of the boat to the Jacuzzi. Again it was a surreal scene. The moon, stars, good food, good music, great company and another first for her a Jacuzzi tubs. Jacob turned on the heat bowl and started taking off his clothes, showing off his very well kept body in swimming trunks and motion for Kya to follow his lead.

They must've sat in the Jacuzzi until they were shivered water-logged prunes. Again the conversation was about their lives, past, future and present. Jacob talked about his marriage and how he felt trapped sometimes. His wife he was sure cared for him and he suspected she even loved him once but now it was all about show and what he can give her; he also talked about his two sons and daughter and how they were just like him. They wanted the support but none of the money and they made it on their own. His oldest son Jacob Jr. own and operated a popular magazine, his daughter Misty worked for a top designer and if fact had designed and produced her own clothing line and the baby boy as he called him, Jack was a quarterback at Alabama State University and was headed to the pros.

Kya talked a little about her friends, the trouble in Ponde and Hurricane Katrina that sent her fleeing for a new life in Little Pebbles. As she began to talk about memories of Bailey, Airis and Chandenise it brought tears to her eyes. Kya ducked her head down quickly so Jacob wouldn't see the tear but he did. Kya tried to shake it off with laugher but the laughter brought more tears. Jacob held her close and just let her get it out. After the crying stop they still held each close and she could smell his masculine cologne and the atmosphere change suddenly.

Jacob must have sensed it too because he start slowly stroking the small of her back as Kya did a surrendering lean into him to gain more closeness. Then as luck would have it one of Kya favorite song came on. Let's get cloooooser, closer than close, let's get cloooooser, closer than most sang Atlantic Starr. The song coupled with the many glasses of champagne she consumed sent her sexually reeling. When Jacob bent down to kiss her she arched her back and gave him a reciprocated kiss forgetting the rules of Merry Ladies which was no sex. Still clad in a wet bathing suits the two of them forgot about their trouble and found solace in kissing, rubbing and touching each other as they clumsily made their way downstairs to the bed. With Atlantic Starr still egging her on to get close, Kya melted when Jacob lifted her up and then placed her down on the bed.

Its lunch time Jacob proclaimed! I can't believe you're still hungry Kya said; we just ate all of that food. Jacob just shook his head as he towered over her in the bed and began to kiss her neck, shoulders, breast, stomach, and upper thigh then back to her navel. No dear, what I seek is not eatable but very tasty and he began to peel off the bottom half of her bathing suit with a steady hand. Kya was tipsy and nervous, she hadn't been with a man since Bruce let along a white man, but she couldn't stop herself. Her monkey was throbbing for the feel and touch of a real banana instead of a battery operated one.

Things were really heating up, just when Kya thought she was losing the battle of sexual control Jacob stopped his lovely assault on her womanly triangle to make things a more cozy and romantic atmosphere. He walked over to the night table and lit a scented candle, then turned and headed for the light switch. That's when Kya lost all of her romantic mood. Dead smack in the top crack of his butt cheeks was a piece of what look like tissue paper, uuuugghh!!

Kya jumped up suddenly to Jacob but to her it was a needed thing. She couldn't decide if she should tell him and which probably cause him embarrassment or say nothing but cite the rules of Merry Ladies; which was no sex! Kya apologized profusely and asked Jacob to take her home as she began to get dress in her still wet bathing bottom. Jacob rushed to her side, placed both hands on her shoulders and asked if he had done something wrong? He said he wasn't trying to pressure her into doing anything she did not want to do. Then as he looked into her eyes he said I will take you anywhere you want to go Kya but for now I will take you home.

During the ride back to Kya's apartment the banter between Kya and Jacob was the same as usual. They were wrapped into each other arms with an occasional kiss in between conversation while listening to one of the many r&b cds Jacob had made for Kya.

Neither even mention what could of happen or why it didn't. Once the limo pulled in front of Kya's place she turned to Jacob and said if only I had met you under different circumstances gave him one mind numbing sloppy kiss and race into the elevator, in her front door threw herself on the sofa. Thank goodness for that square or two of quilted soft Northern or she would be in a lot of trouble.

Another Way of Seeing the Easy

Saturday morning and Kya was still on the couch, after the night she almost had she just couldn't get up so the sofa was a great place for slumber. As Kya reach to turn on the lamp on the end table there was a knock at the door. It was Babette twelve years old daughter Ty; she wanted to know if Kya had seen her mom. Ty said her mom left to go to the local store last night around ten and she hadn't seen her since. She wasn't concern at first because well Babette was known to leave overnight but was there first thing in the morning to feed the kids.

Kya told Ty to bring the little ones over to her apartment for some cereal and milk while they call around to her usual hang out and then assured Ty that her mother was ok. After closing the door Kya felt to her knees to pray that Babette was ok because she was a good mother even if her means weren't the best way to support her family. Quickly she had to at least brush her teeth and wash her face before her apartment was bombarded with little ones scurrying about.

As soon as little Shayla and Shanna was in the door they wanted to know if they were going to bake cookies, ten year old Terry wanted to know where he could plug in his video game and his five year old brother Marcus just wanted to eat. Neither of children had a clue of the worry Ty and Kya had for their mother; hopefully Babette would be found before they knew anything was a missed.

Its three pm and no Babette, Ty had called her grandmother earlier that day and they came to pick up the kids but Kya was still worried. The police said it had to be twenty four hours before they could even start looking for her especially since she had a history of leaving. Kya was thinking that she didn't need the added stress as she cleaned up the mess of making homemade cookies with the kids. She had to do something but she also had to relax for her date tonight with Laverna which was a task in itself.

Kya decided to fore go her normal work out and just sit on her patio to see if Babette skinny body would appear with her brew in tow. So far all she saw was Jackson and his gang of friends sitting on the street corner and their usual shenanigans for money was going on. Jackson would dance while his buddy Matt would blow a tune into a bucket. Their buddies Chris and Joe were clacking along with spoons as the people would leave dribs and drabs of their hard earn money in a cigar box for entertainment. They actually made enough money to buy their jolly juice for a day.

Shoot its seven o'clock now and Kya had to do something to perk herself up and what better way than a drink while soaking in a tub of bubbles. She decided she would put Babette out of her mind for now and concentrate on what to tell Laverna. She needed the money and was willing to be a companion but the sex part would be something she couldn't get with, hopefully that would be enough for her and she won't make a stir with Merry Ladies.

Tonight's attire a tangerine mini skirt with a short sleeve jacket, off white halter and for a dramatic affect she tied a green and tangerine scarf around her neck. Laverna wanted to meet at the local theater for a play then a seafood meal afterwards. Kya longed for seafood; she hadn't had good boiled crawfish or shrimps since leaving home. So tonight she had planned to be greedy because Laverna didn't do anything but the best of everything she did.

As always Laverna delivered on the good time. They took a plane to New Orleans and did up the town. It felt different to Kya to be there as a tourist but she couldn't or wouldn't let Laverna know her past. They visit Pat O'Brian in the French quarters and drank the biggest Hurricane ever, ate a delicious meal at the Court of Two Sisters and in a surprise Laverna said lets go gamble and they ended up at Harrah's Casino.

Laverna played the black jack table like a pro. She hit twenty one more often than the men swooned around her and knew when to freeze. Next was the roulette table and she was winning big time. Kya was in awe of this woman, could she do nothing great. Now the concierge where offering the women free rooms and Laverna took them up on it. They had a huge two bedroom suite with a breath taking view of the crescent city from the balcony. Kya concern was that she didn't have a change of clothes or toiletries and in her sensual voice Laverna said to her, haven't you learned anything baby. I can get us anything now relax I won't try anything, at least not tonight she laughed as she entered her bedroom.

Awakening the next morning groggy from the huge hurricane drink, Kya remembered she was in the comfortable hotel room at the casino. She turned over to the bay window and saw a clothing bag from Macy draped across the chair. Kya jumped out of bed and unzipped the bag to reveal a stunning coral dress. On the night table was a box with the necessary under garments and accessories. Wow Laverna out did herself with this, Kya was thinking she could definitely get use to stuff like that.

Just as Kya finish dressing Laverna knocked at the door saying breakfast time. Kya walked into the sitting room to find a buffet of fruits, hot cakes, croissants, bacon, sausages along with different types of breakfast drinks like coffee and orange juice. Laverna was chowing down on scramble eggs, crepes and strawberries with Canadian bacon then she poured herself a glass of mango orange juice and added some champagne; emphasis on the champagne. To Kya it was cold, smooth and delicious looking and she asked Laverna how did it taste? It's called a Mimosa and it's sinfully good; have some she replied.

The two ladies spent the rest of Sunday touring New Orleans like two longtime friends. There was lunch on the paddleboat the Creole Queen, extensive shopping at the New Orleans Centre and one more go at the casino where Kya herself won quite a bit of money playing the slot machines. Kya was having so much fun, too much probably but who cared Kya thought, I just won enough money to buy me a new car. So she weaved her way back to the black jack table where a crowd had formed.

Of course it was Laverna and she was commanding attention yet again, she was playing her hands at ten thousand a pop. Laverna had a queen of spades showing and the dealer was showing an eight of club. He flipped the Laverna's facedown card and it was an eight of spade. He then turned the tables' second card and it was a ten of diamond. The crowed just owed and awed but as cool as a cucumber Laverna motioned for the dealer to hit her. Kya eyes bucked out of their sockets when the three of hearts flip on the table; another twenty thousand. Luck of the two ladies Laverna said and she pointed to the queen of spade on the table and then turned to Kya kiss her on the lips and handed her the chips.

They made their way back to the casino hotel to pack. Laverna asked Kya to have a seat first because she needed to talk with her. Kya heart was sitting squarely in her throat as Laverna started with the twenty thousand is yours to keep regardless and although we are not in Vegas what we do here stays here. We have been pussy footing around our attraction to each other all day. I will take care of things with your job and Mr. Barrows on tomorrow and even pay you double what you make in a day if you would spend the night in my room. Laverna said "Kya just ten minutes in my arms is all I ask and once we go to our separate rooms if you feel you can venture further my door will be open. No strings attached."

Kya was tired of fighting the attraction too. She felt brazen and moved directly into Laverna's arm. It felt good to Kya yet familiarly strange as she place her head on top of those cushiony DD. Laverna at first hugged her like she was consoling a little girl, then once Kya looked into her eyes Laverna began to kiss her. Soft feathery pecks at first then as she slid her tongue into her mouth the kiss became more aggressive as if she was trying to find something or cure a hunger. Kya found herself melting like butter at the touch of this woman. Laverna was the first to break the embrace and simply walked into her room leaving the door slightly a jarred.

The Move

⁓

Returning home Monday from New Orleans, Kya learned that Babette was safe. She told Kya that she intended to go to the nearest emergency room overnight and be home before the kids woke up. She knew she was pregnant and started spotting that evening, she figured she wouldn't mention it to the kids if there was a chance of a miscarriage. Babette thought she would have the D&C, back home and no one would be the wiser. Instead it was a bigger issue; it seems she will be having another set of twins. Poor Babette!

"Oh don't cry for me!" Babette said as she rummaged through the assortment of new clothes and trinkets Kya still had in shopping bags. My stubbornness to take care of me and my own his put me in this situation but with patience and love we will be alright. Besides my parents are willing to help me out and they are starting by letting me move in their rental house on McKinley rent free. It comes with conditions of course; I have to go back to college, pay my own utilities, get my personal life in order and oh yeah some type of birth control. No worries my friend, I will be fine and I will keep in touch with you because I want you to be the godmother. Kya agreed to that notion.

Kya and Babette talked all about Kya's trip to the big easy and almost all the things she did there. She even told Babette how Laverna betted ten thousand on blackjack split the king got an ace on both and won twenty. Wow Babette said, what does she do for a living?

Kya was saved from answering that question by the ringing of her phone; the caller ID said Juane'. She didn't need anyone knowing of the deeds that would raise any questions about the bank and fore more Merry Ladies. The last things Kya heard Babette say as she was leaving Kya alone to her phone call "was it must be good to have a friend like that, I'm going finish moving we'll chat later."

Juane showed up at Kya's door around five fifteen. Her eyes said do tell all Kya Martinley as she plopped down on the sofa and started flicking the station on Kya new plasma TV. Just as anxious as she was on the phone earlier she wanted details and all the juicy tidbits. Kya reached into her purse and slammed the two straps of hundreds down on the coffee table between them. "Damn girl what did you have to do for that?" "Nothing" Kya said, Laverna is just a lonely woman who likes my friendship. Juane' sprouted "Did she buy you that plasma screen too, that thing almost takes up the whole wall?" Kya mumbled No, I bought that myself. The only thing I ask of you Juane' is not to breathe a word to anyone about the money, please! "Mums the word girl, I got you now let's see what goodies you brought back" was all Juane' said.

After rummaging through the shopping bag showing off the expensive dresses, lingerie, shoes and jewelry acquired on her trip Kya asked "Juane you hungry? I haven't eaten since early this morning and a sista is hungry." Sure girl I'm down for a dinner if you are treating and besides I can fill you in on what happened at work today with Nykole and Mr. Barrow squealed Juane'. "We can go to that new restaurant on Fourteenth Street called Replica of N.O. I hear it has some really good soul food and I know you miss good red beans and rice."

En-route to the restaurant the ladies dished about Juane' kids, Mr. Sweaty who is one of Juane's clients and all the crazy customers that came through the bank that day but once seated the subject turned to Nykole. "Man Kya she has got it in for you, Juane' revealed when Mr. Barrow announced you weren't coming in today she went off on a tirade for about an hour, even after we had customers you could hear her and Mr. Barrows shouting in his office. The argument spilled into the lobby and onward to Nykole office. Mr. Barrow reminded her that he was in charge and with that left Nykole's office and the bank for the day. Nykole slammed the door so hard it shook the adjacent teller station. Barbara came up with the nickname slammy because lately that's all Nykole seem to be doing is slamming doors and with each slam her station was falling apart." The two laughed at that notion and ordered the red bean and rice special.

"Juane would you give me a ride after work on tomorrow to meet with the manager of the Hillside Townhouses," Kya asked. Hell I had to weigh the pro and cons of what I needed to do first, move or buy a car and I think moving won. "Sure girl said Juane', beside you won't be too far from me and maybe we can have a sleep over or something and talk about Queen Nykole. You know sometimes I feel like I'm back in high school, you know when the most popular girl get thrown off her throne she gets feisty and think of all kinds of ways to get back on top."

After dinner Juane' dropped Kya back off at her apartment. Kya went inside to enjoy the luxurious TV she purchased about a month ago. She had never actually turned the plasma on because she wanted to wait and enjoy it at her new townhouse that she hope would be approved soon. Since Babette had already started moving her things out of the four-plex and spending time at her new home Kya figured it would get lonely during the week with no twins to bake cookies with or Babette to tell her gossip and keep her abreast of the latest trends.

Now the weekend was something totally different. Jacob and Laverna occupied a lot of her time and if truth be told Kya was enjoying every aspect of it. "Ugh! Except the tissue that was wedge in between Jacob ass!" Kya said out loud. She hoped he never ask her what happen because she didn't want to tell the old coot it would probably embarrass him to death but he did have a great ass for a man of his age. Now Laverna was a different story, Kya found that she like being in her company and who wouldn't, the woman is extraordinary. She is beautiful, funny and rich. She didn't ask for much just to spend some time with her and Kya get to see things she has already seen in a new light. She was like a female version of Bruce.

Bruce she hadn't thought about him in several months. She walked over to her computer desk to retrieve the two letters that was forward in the mail once she moved to Little Pebble. She opens the first one with the earliest postmark. It read:

Dear Kya

It seems we have made a mess of things. As I have told you before, I have always admired you from a far and when that night happened it was like a dream come true. I know I was wrong for taking advantage of you because you were drunk and lonely but I just couldn't help myself.

By now you are aware of my pending baby and yes I just couldn't bring myself to tell you that I was drunk and let my long head do the thinking for me. It was a one night stand and unlike our relationship I have regretted it.

In the beginning Chandenise was a beautiful, fun woman. Then in just six months her true color came shining through. I was blind to it at first then more and more she wanted thing and threaten to leave if I didn't get them for her. People don't know that side of our relationship. They don't know that she would nag, whine and bitch to no end. You guys saw a relationship that was perfect but if you look closer you would see I was hurting and she was enjoying every bit of it.

Well I just wanted to write a few words to you and hope you would come visit me soon.

Love Bruce

PS, I have my lawyers draw up a will and get my finance in order so soon you will be receiving a check from me. If you will please make sure the money gets divided in three parts. I would like for one third to go to Ms. Grainger for the baby, the second third to Lois for Kenya and the last third to you.

Please honey think about coming to see me, it would make this place easier to bear if I knew soon I would be looking into your beautiful eyes even if it's through plexi-glass.

Again Love Bruce

Kya just folded the letter and placed it back into the envelope. She couldn't bring herself to read the other letter so she put both back into her desk drawer. She would have to find out what's going on with Ms. Grainger and the baby and see that Bruce wishes are carried out. She didn't want her share so she decided to split the money between the two, the unborn baby and Kenya. She wasn't going to let herself think about it as she walked to the bathroom to take a shower, she did her normal routine turned on the bathroom radio, cleansed her face, turn on the shower and soon as the water trickled on her body she laid her forehead on the shower tiles and started crying. A deep soul crying that left her wetter than the water coming from the shower head with trembles and all. Kya did a quick wash, rinse, dry and threw herself under the covers to cry some more.

The morning found Kya wide awake and emotionally drained. She just lugged herself around the house getting ready for work. Before she left Kya knelt on her knees to talk with God because who knows your heart better than he. It had to be some kind of way to clear her heavy heart so she could continue to move forward in life. She has a great job and second job with the Merry Ladies and soon she would be moving into a great townhouse so life has been good to her even though she probably don't deserve it. She knew it was guilt and it was eating away at her soul but then she thought about Chandenise and how she mistreated Bruce and the guilt would yet again be buried in the back folder of her heart marked sorry. She will have to deal with the grief some other time because Juane has just parked outside and honking her horn like a crazy woman. Kya grabbed her purse and jacket, locked her door and by the time she reached the car all was well with her.

Juane and Kya approached the bank just as the candy red ford escape was pulling out of the parking lot. Juane didn't notice a thing but Kya did, it's the second time she has come upon the vehicle and Mr. Barrow's car was sitting in his parking space meaning he was already inside and conducted his business with the person in the tripped out ride. He greeted the ladies as the security guard Captain Lewis opened the door for them and went straight into his office slamming the door. "Oh boy Juane' said it's going to be a hell of a day. Mr. Barrows seems to be in a bad mood already." Captain Lewis walked over to Kya and whispered "how are you today sexy lady?" Kya didn't know how to respond so she went on preparing for work like she didn't hear him.

Once Nykole, Dominicki and Barbara arrived Mr. Barrows came out for the morning huddle. He informed all that they have met their teamwork goal again and that the payout will be on the next check as usual. He also mention that they went from 100 % to 98% in the gallup polls so whatever little tiffs that are going on behind the teller line needs to be fixed and we move on from there to go back up to the one hundred percentile and with that he turned giving Nykole a very stern look before going back into his office.

The first customer through the door was one of the banks usual complainers Mrs. Legrew she is a sweet old lady of seventy that still haven't grasp the concept of balancing her check book since her husband death two years ago. Dominicki had the pleasure of helping her; going through her checkbook registry check by check to see where she went wrong and explaining to her that because it wasn't a bank error that the bank couldn't refund her NSF fee. Of course she went on a yelling spree and promised to close her account before leaving. The day went by pretty smooth after Mrs. Legrew left. Nonstop of people coming in to cash checks, make deposit or pay on whatever loan they possessed with the bank. Kya couldn't wait until the door was closed so she could go on to hopefully sign a lease to her new townhouse.

Looks Promising

After work Juane' dropped Kya off at the Hillside Townhouses to meet with the office manager. Since she lived in the neighboring townhouses up the street so Juane' headed home to check on her kids telling Kya to call her once she was done. The manager introduced himself as Willie and he and Kya went over the rules of the townhouse in full details, he handed her the keys and they both walked over to HT3. On the walk over he showed Kya where all of the recreation rooms were, the pools and unwanted little tidbits about her neighbors in HT1, HT2 and HT4 which Kya didn't even care because she was leaving the four-plex.

Once they were inside the door Kya was confronted with a big spacious living-room, off to the left was the kitchen and back door leading to a mid-size backyard with storage shed. Back into the house Kya went upstairs to see her enormous bedroom and bath. She asked Willie to forgive her but she just had to lie on the plush rug and do rug angels for a few minutes. He led Kya back down the stairs to show her the big closet and half bathroom under the stairwell before leaving her alone. As giddy as a lamb Kya called Juane' up to bring her home.

After touring her new townhouse Juane' promised Kya she would take her furniture shopping on Saturday morning "so don't stay out to late with McFarland on Friday night," Juane' said when she dropped Kya at the four-plex. Kya didn't get on the elevator to her apartment instead she just stood in the yard looking at what will be her past. Indeed the place had its good and bad but Kya was in need of a change. Then she thought about Ms. Poers, she had to visit her. Since she started working at the bank Kya hadn't really visited her in a while just saw her in passing as either one was coming or going about. Ms. Poers was very nice to Kya when she first moved in so Kya wanted to be the one to tell her she was moving out.

The old lady answered the door looking extremely tired. She apologized to Kya for all the loud music stating that her fifteen year old granddaughter has found a new love in some new rap singer. "Every time I ask her to turn it down it eventually gets turned back up. Well at least it's not that foul mouth Lil Weed, Weenzy or whatever his name is, child I can't keep up with all of them," Ms. Poers chuckled.

Have a seat my dear and as the kids say what's up? Kya told Ms. Poers about her moving and that she was going to miss her very much; she rose to hug Ms. Poers across the table and leg gave away causing the table and homemade center piece to crash to the floor. "Ms. Poers I'm so sorry!" Kya cried out but the old lady told her not to worry about it she would just get another stick and prop the old thing back up. "Good luck to you and don't be a stranger, I will miss our talks the most," then the old lady closed the door to complain again to her granddaughter about the loud music.

Kya went inside and grabbed her back pack filled with the twenty thousand Laverna gave her in New Orleans. She pulled out her calculator to tally up first, last and security deposit along with the cost of renting a truck, buying a house full of furniture and possibly some new clothes. Nah, scrap the clothes Kya thought, I will give Ms. Poers the money I had earmarked for clothes as she put two thousand dollars in an envelope. She will be too proud to take it so once my last box is on the truck I will put the envelope in the mail slot and drive away. Kya then put on her music and started what little packing she could because it was at least nine thirty and she had to prepare for bed but first a little celebratory drink was in order.

Wednesday then Thursday came with Kya not caring what Nykole put her through at work because she was on a high. She would be moving on Saturday and that alone was enough motivation for her to ignore the evil woman at least until the Merry Ladies meeting that evening but until that time comes Kya was going to enjoy a medi/pedi at "Hoofs and Foots" then on to Lacey's salon to have her full lace wig washed and condition for tomorrow's meeting with the big country coot Jacob. Thing were never dull with him and he promise to top things this weekend because he was taking her on an overnight stay but where his email didn't say.

As her feet soak in a tub of spraying hot water Kya began calculating her money again, let's see she thought twenty thousand from Laverna, one thousand the first weekend with Merry Ladies and two thousand the next weekend. Paycheck pays all the household bills, like food, cable, water, gas, cell phone and internet services. So all the extra money was free and clear to buy furniture of course minus the four thousand fifty dollars she need for the townhouse and the two thousand she sat aside for Ms. Poers.

Wally's was jumping as always when the group got there. Barbara and Dominicki were complaining about work again as they were being seated, Mr. Barrows seemed to be in another place, Nykole dug out a mirror to check her hair and make-up while Juane' and Kya glance over the drink menu, they both wanted something they had not tried before and the menu at Wally's had so many dishes and drinks you could go there for two months and still eat something new. George the waiter came over to see if the group wanted the usual, everyone said yes except Juane' and Kya. Juane' said she wanted to try the brainstorm drink with crab stuff shrimps and Kya order the rib-eye steak with stuffed cappers and wild rice and a lollygag drink.

With hors d'oeuvres and drinks severed it was time for the meeting to begin. This time Nykole started off the meeting by saying Merry Ladies has a new client, his name is Jordan McMillian and he owns a sleuth of furniture stores all over the world. He is here this weekend and will be back in town in four weeks looking for a date to the annual Arkansas Ball. I of course will be his first engagement and the chain of command between you four will be in accordance for the next ones until he decides whom he likes best."

"Next order of cheery business, Mr. Barrow said "its payday and also I want to celebrate another year of Merry Ladies and thanks to all of you old and new that has made it a success. Remember ladies no sex, I don't care what gifts or monetary value that is offered we stay just above legal that way by saying no." Mr. Barrows told Kya she was excuse from work tomorrow, McFarland will be picking you up around noon so don't disappoint him. Now if there is no more order of business eat, drink and be merry and then Mr. Barrows did something no one had heard from him before; a deep throated chuckle. Then he said "ladies I don't know about you but I am enjoying this ride for however long it last and I suggest you do the same. I going home now, it's my mother-in-law birthday so the wife is expecting me soon so goodnight."

With Mr. Barrows gone Nykole adjourned the meeting and damn near knocked Kya out of her chair when she bumped into it in a huff to leave. Barbara, Dominicki, Juane and Kya laughed at the assistant manager/queen bee. "Poor thing Barbara said, she can't stand someone out doing her in any manner; she either has bad dreams, want to royally whip your ass or has a dart board with your picture on it Kya. Do you feel any holes in your face? Ladies let's get out of here and see you next week Kya, have fun!" Kya just laughed at Barbara's words and replied "girl you are just as crazy as the rest of us and thanks I will have fun, you guys need to be careful tomorrow Slammy will most definitely be in a bad mood." Kya chimed in. Then the ladies paid the bill even Nykole part because her leaving mad was repayment enough for them.

"So since your off tomorrow what are you going to do?" Juane' asked Kya. Kya responded by saying, "tonight I will pack a few more things I want to take with me, I'm leaving most of my crappy furniture for the next tenant they may be starting over and need it. Then I'm going to shave all the hairy spots on my body and go to bed early because I'm not sure what Jacob has plan." Juane' quip in "Whatever it is you need the day off to do it, but don't forget I will be here around eleven Saturday to take you shopping so be ready I have a couple of places that I think suits your taste." Kya assured Juane' she would be ready and headed inside.

Kya grabbed the mail from the mailbox and sat on the sofa; she skimmed the envelope and froze when she came upon one that read Ponde Correctional Facilities. Damn, it didn't have a yellow forwarding sticker on it so how did Bruce find her was the thought running through her mind? Kya didn't even open the letter she just put it with the other two in her desk drawer. She was determined to leave that part behind her because she was tired of crying and saying what ifs. As the old saying goes "if IF was a fifth we would all be drunk" and tonight Kya wanted to be sober.

It's the big day and because McFarland was being so secretive Kya had no idea what to wear. After her normal routine of preparation she opted for a pair of blue jeans and dressed them up with a light blue lace camisole, medium blue linen jacket, red bottom taupe heels and matching purse. Now for the hair Kya said to herself, she tried many styles but in the end she swept her long lace wig in a sideways ponytail fastened by a multicolored butterfly clip. Nothing left to do but wait on Jacob, maybe a drink will settle my nerves but just as she reach the bottle of patron the doorbell rang. She opened the door to Jacob and what seemed like his entourage and they were carrying all types of packages.

Get ready for the night of your beautiful life Jacob told Kya, these ladies are here to prepare you. I will wait in the living room but put a little pep in your step we have to be on the plane by noon. Kya showed the ladies the way to the bathroom when the littlest of the trio asked. Once there she plugged in a flat iron and set up all kinds of hair products, the second one set out all types of make-up and the third laid out four of the most elegant dresses for Kya to choose from. In the end Kya choose a Donna Karan silk organza and haboti patchwork v-neck dress with a pair of Donna Karan Galactic strapped sandals. After having her make-up and hair done Kya was ready, she nervously entered the living room but once she saw the gleam in Jacob's eye when he saw her; all her apprehension went away.

They arrived at the airport a few minutes ahead of schedule so the pair waited in the airport lounge, where people were falling over themselves to be at Jacob beck and call. "Jacob this almost feels like that scene in "Pretty Woman" Kya said, with a few exceptions of course and I got to tell you I love it." Nothing but the best for you my dear now our Lear jet awaits as he held out his hand to her while tipping his hat. They walked armed and armed to the jet and once seated Jacob told Kya they were going Ballas, Texas. Kya was excited, she had never been to Ballas, Texas but Nykole bragged about the good eating and shopping there all the time. Jacob could see that questioning look on Kya's face so he spoke up saying we are going to have dinner, cocktails and stay in the finest hotel.

Welcome Mr. McFarland and Ms. Martinley we should touched down at the BFW airport around three, the pilot announced. During the ride there Kya and Jacob decided to get some sleep, Kya laid her head on Jacob's shoulders and took in the manly aroma of him. He had broad shoulders, six pack abs, and what she could tell from their yacht trip he was well endowed too. Damn why couldn't they have met differently and he not be married. Why do I have such bad luck with men, either they are married or jackasses as Kya mentally questioned herself.

Then she thought shake it off fool you are in Ballas, Texas with a rich older white man who either adores you or is a very good actor in any case get it together before you ruin things. Once the plane landed the pair walked off the plane hand in hand into an awaiting limo, the first stop was to Jabco's an elite hotel in downtown Ballas. Jacob had the best penthouse reserved for just the two of them.

It had a large living area, full size kitchen and two master suites and a Jacuzzi on the balcony. Kya walked into her bedroom, it's was big and beautiful. There was a king size bed, forty inch flat screen and plenty of closet space. Kya opened one of the closet doors and found more clothes, shoes and accessories waiting for her. There was a note on her pillow instructing her to pick out what ensemble that she like because they were going dine in style, so rest up little filly and be ready by seven sharp. Since I know that will be hard for you I arranged for a masseuse to come help you relax, see you soon Jacob.

Nykole the Interrupter

~~~~~

That was so sweet of him Kya thought let me go thank him. As she made her way across the living area to Jacob's room there was a knock at the door. She made a detour to answer and it was room service with a light snacking of cheese, crackers and champagne, follow by the masseuse and bellman holding a beautiful bouquet of lilies. Kya told the masseuse Ms. Lopez to go ahead and set up she would be right back and she rushed over Jacob's room only to find the he wasn't there. It kind of disappointed her but she knew she would be able to express her feeling during dinner.

Now lying naked on the stretched out table Ms. Lopez placed a towel over her bottom area and began to slowly knead her calves down to her feet. She massaged and cracked Kya's toes, worked her way back up to her buttock, back, shoulders and arms and followed the massage with a complete rub down of warming lotion. It felt like heaven, Kya couldn't have been more relaxed. In fact she was ready to sleep but she knew she had to go and decide on a dress to wear. She tried on a Vera Wang cris-cross dressed in apple green, a canary yellow Donna Karan wrap dress and multi-colored loosely hung in the front and back dress by Coco Channel. Decision, decision, decision what the hell to wear Kya was twirling around laughing at her predicament.

It's now five-forty seven, Kya is now bathe and still undecided what to wear. She looked over the wardrobe again and opted for the multi-colored dress because it was the one that made her feel the sexiest. At Jacob's request the hotel sent up a make-up artist and stylist to do her hair and make-up. Kya didn't have to lift a finger sort to speak they made a production out of everything. The stylist recommended that she wear her own hair instead of the wig; styling her hair in a French twist, with a couple of curls hanging just below the temple. As she looked herself over in the mirror she loved what stared back. Her hair immaculate and her makeup looked as if she wasn't wearing any with the exception of the garnet red lipstick and smoky eyes. As everyone cleared up their belongings Kya got dressed.

Transformed and ready Kya waited for her date to emerge from his room. She was nervous so she walked onto the balcony to catch a breath of fresh air. Ballas, Texas was beautiful. Kya could see the famous amusement parks, hotels and restaurants all lit up. Standing there enjoying the breeze and a drink she smelled him before he approached the area, Kya took in a good whiff of his masculine cologne sending shivers through her body. She turned to see that Jacob was dressed in a dark navy Armani suit with a multi-colored tie that complimented her dress. For the first time that Kya could remember he wasn't wearing a cowboy hat, she always figured that the hat was part of his height, charm and looks but he was still tall and quite handsome without it.

Jacob whistled his approval of her appearance as Kya made her way to his waiting arms. They took the limo to dinner at Bodega where the scene was intimate, quiet and soft music. Once seated McFarland asked Kya if he mind if he ordered for them, after her agreement he order tuna tar-tar with beluga caviar for appetizers. After the waiter left with their entrée order of Porterhouse steak with sautéed mushroom, new potatoes and a Cesar salad, Kya excused herself and went to the ladies room. Upon her return she spotted two additional people at the table. The man she didn't recognize but the woman was that she devil Nykole. Oh! Goodness how and why is she here of all places was all Kya keeping saying to herself as she made her way back to her seat.

As Jacob stood up to pull out Kya's chair he made the introductions. "Kya this is my good friend Jordan McMillian and his date, I'm sorry honey, what's your name again?" McFarland asked Nykole. Over vaseline glided teeth Nykole repeated her name. "Well everybody this is Kya, the beautifully fabulous young lady I was telling you about a moment ago. She has made this old stallion happy again just by gracing me with her presence and tonight I intend to show her my appreciation by showing her a great time," was all McFarland said.

That made Kya's night she was blushing and grinning from ear to ear while Nykole sat there stewing because she wasn't the center of attention. Despite the fact that Nykole made every attempt to show Kya up, like pointing out she was using the wrong fork to eat her salad with and her napkin should be draped over her lap and not across her chest. To save face McFarland tucked his napkin in his collar too and doted over Kya like they were a real couple and she wasn't a paid date.

The rest of the night went smoothly for the two couples, after dinner they went to Vino's for drinks then over to "Hotstept" one of Ballas, Texas premier dance spot. Jordan and Nykole dance a little but Jacob McFarland swirled Kya on the dance floor with sensuous ease. They were the talk of the dance floor and Kya was even impressed with Jacob when he actually did his rendition of the duggie. It was a hilarious valiant try, as most of the dancer laughed at Jacob he kept going even with his bones creaking and cracking. Jacob knew he was making a mess of the whole dance but Kya was important to him and she wanted to duggie. So duggie he did!

The evening ended with Jacob and Kya saying goodnight to Jordan and Nykole. Nykole protested but McMillian got the hint that Jacob wanted to be alone with Kya so he told Nykole they were going to St. Martin's Wine Bistro for more drinks. He kissed Kya on the cheek while saying it was nice to meet her and shook Jacob hand telling him he was a lucky man. That hit a nerve with the queen bee; she asked Jordan what the hell you mean by that? Jordan reply was nothing my dear Nykole you speak for yourself was the last thing Kya heard McMillian tell Nykole before she and Jacob horse and carriage trotted away.

Back at the hotel, Jacob said he was getting into the hot tub and asked Kya to join him. Kya said she was going to call it a night and went to her room. Jacob had a sad look on his tan face but understood. "Ok little lady, have sweet dream, I'm going soak awhile," with that Jacob went into his room. Kya sat on the bed thinking, she really did enjoy her time with Jacob. He treated her like a queen; she looked around the expensive room and all the clothes and stuff bought especially for her. He made sure she had everything and asked for nothing but a little more time. What the heck I'm going in the Jacuzzi but he is going to see the real me. She washed the makeup off her face, put her hair in a ponytail after showering, put on one of the expensive looking bathing suits and headed to the balcony.

Jacob was sitting there in the hot tub with his eyes close holding a drink and listening to r&b music. Kya quietly stepped in not to disturb him. It was hot, exhilarating, and relaxing. She laid back closed her eyes too and listen to the music. Drink my dear is what Kya suddenly heard, she open her eyes to a smiling Jacob. "Sure why not, it's beautiful out here Jacob I see why you like it here," was Kya reply. Jacob said with a grin "Yeah that and I own this swanky place, now relax and my I say you look glowing and marvelous." That made Kya grin like a school girl which seems to happen a lot when she was with him. Brain McKnight "find myself in you" came on the radio, as the two talked past all the sexual tension luring in the air. Kya was getting hornier with each sip of patron she drank and Jacob eyes said the same.

They ran out of small talk and Kya hadn't realized that either she got closer to Jacob or he sat closer to her but the heat between what little space they had was like a big roaring fireball. Kya decide enough was enough as she rose; straddle Jacob lap and they began to kiss. Appropriately "Don't disturb this groove" by The System came soaring through the speakers and Kya took heed to the words.

Jacob knocked on Kya's door early that Saturday morning. Wake up sleepy head let's eat this marvelous spread of croissants, sausage, eggs, and all the things I thought you would like. Ok, just let me finish packing I will be out in a minute was Kya reply. Opening the door with her suitcase in tow Kya saw Jacob at the table eating a big hearty breakfast, her first words was thanks for a lovely night it would be something she will always remember then sat at the table to pancakes and canadian bacon. When Kya reached for the syrup she spotted a box with her name on it. She looked over a Jacob and he said no thank you. They made the trip back to Little Pebble with smiles and memories.

Greed her Undoing

Kya made it home in just enough time to throw her suit cases in the house and hop in the car with Juane'. They went to an exclusive furniture store on the north side of town that caterer to the rich. Kya lost her mind, she bought a king size padded headboard bedroom set with two night stands and lamp, a cherry wood dinette with six chairs and matching armoire, a black and white leather section that had two lazy boys chairs along with the matching coffee table and ends, two standing silver lamps, a med-size bar complete with ice maker and wine rack then her final purchase was a complete stereo system with a large capacity cd rack all to be delivered on that Monday evening.

After shopping and a quick lunch with Juane' they both made it back to the four-plex to pack up the last of the things Kya was taking with her. As they settle down to read the classified Kya was hoping she can find a nice car she could afford. "Not much money left after my morning shopping spree but the good thing is we get paid Thursday from Merry Ladies and the bank on Friday; until then I will have to either bum a ride from you or hop on the bus," Kya told Juane'. "girl you know that's no problem, but if you want me too I can call up my friend Stanley over at Diamond to see if he can get you a deal on a nice car?" Juane asked. Hell thanks Juane' I really would appreciate it, you're a life saver was Kya comment. "That's what friends are for," Juane' replied as she was leaving out the door.

Friends, Kya hope she could be a better friend to Juane than she was to Chandenise. The truth is things were not supposed to happen like it did. She had to get it off her chest she just didn't know how without telling the one person who deemed her a friend, she couldn't risk Juane' knowing what secrets she kept and ran from nope that she will keep to herself she thought. Now it's time to rest up for the luscious and vivacious Laverna but first she needed to jot last night adventure in her journal. Kya woke up around six and she was running late because she had to meet Laverna at eight o'clock and she couldn't show up less than stunning. She forgo the exercise but did take her usual drink of crown royal with water and a splash of lemon juice while listening to the late Whitney Houston ultimate cd collection.

Kya manage to get to Snails about five minutes before Laverna arrived. Of course she was all that any woman could be dressed in a purple and gray off the shoulder Liz Claiborne that had a split all the way up to her hip which led Kya to believe that she couldn't have on any panties. Before she sat down she gave Kya kiss on the cheek then complimented her on the ensemble she was wearing stating "red is definitely your color". Kya smiled and returned the compliment. "Kya would you like to come over to my place, everyone is gone to Vegas and you can have your own room or stay in mines, your pick. Beside my kitchen is stock and we can have a lovely discreet time?" Laverna asked.

Once again Kya found herself on a private plane only this time she was headed to Tallaways, Alabama. The trip only took an hour but in that time Kya manage to tell Laverna about her moving to a better place and her shopping trip to buy what kind of furniture she wanted courtesy of her. She also mention to Laverna how good it felt to buy what she wanted and not what she could afford. Laverna replied that's good you did something constructive with the money honey glad I could help." They drove a rental over to Laverna mansion and it was as stunning as its owner.

It had a winding drive way that leads to the front door of a tan bricked three story home with what looks like crystal glass shutters on the windows, an abundance of large oak trees that seem to throw plenty of shade and several rows of beautiful azalea perch on both side of the front door. At the back of the house was small man made pond with a gazebo in the center, large pool with adjacent hot tub, full black top for basketball, a full tennis court, a two bedroom guest house, an outside laundry facility that was almost as big as Kya whole apartment and a four car garage that housed Laverna's limo, fully loaded butter crème Denali and red Lincoln Town Car.

The inside was immaculately clean the first floor was where the living room, kitchen and four bedrooms for family and friends were located, the third floor was where the maid, butler, driver and cook lived along with several rooms for storage but the third floor was the coups de grace; a full movie theatre and bowling alley. She had all the latest movies and some that hadn't hit the cinema yet with a full concession featuring nachos, popcorn, hot dogs, junior mints, all different types of candies and a soda fountain; in other words the works. Kya couldn't wait to relax and watch a good movie that was something she hadn't done in years.

After completing the full tour of the house Laverna led Kya back to the guesthouse, it late so get some rest but if you are not tired I will be in the theater in thirty minutes. Before walking away Laverna said "tonight's feature is "Good Deeds", Tyler sent an advance copy over this morning but it doesn't hit the movie theater until Friday and I'm dying to watch it." Kya response was "heck me too, give me a moment to freshen up and I'm there!" Kya had to go to the bathroom and she was glad Laverna decided to put her in the guesthouse because she would probably cleared the place with the storm that was brewing in her stomach knocking to get out, I do hope there is some air freshener were Kya's thoughts as she ran from door to door until she found the correct room plopping down just in time glad that she didn't embarrass herself.

She arrived just in time the movie was just beginning. Laverna was sitting there all comfortable with a large plate of nachos with ground beef, melted and shredded cheese, sour cream and jalapeño peppers with the choice of guacamole and salsa. After watching "Good Deeds" they watched "Safe House" starring Denzel Washington while grubbing on a fully loaded pizza and chugging

Budweiser light beer. Laverna ask Kya if she wanted to watch one of her favorite movie after Kya shook her head yes, Laverna programed all of Martin Lawrence movies and a few of his comedy acts to play back to back. Then she pressed a couple of buttons and the big two front row seats somehow turned into a full comfortable bed.

They laughed and laughed really enjoying the movies as if it was the first time they saw it. Kya said "it really feels good to just be loose sometime isn't it, no make-up, fancy clothes and hair flowing free." Laverna nodded her head but she was distance and Kya could tell but was to chicken to ask her what was wrong. As if she was reading Kya's mind Laverna said she was getting sleepy but Kya was more than welcome to continue to watch whatever she like but she was going to bed. Kya didn't want to be there alone so she asked Laverna to stay. "Besides these beds are pretty comfortable and I promise I won't laugh to loud." Kya pleaded.

Alright Kya, I will be right back was all Laverna said as she went to the closet at the back of the entertainment room to retrieve bedding then call over the intercom for the Stacey one of her maids to come and make up the beds. When Stacey came in the room you could tell she wasn't too happy being woken up at two thirty in the morning to make beds. As Laverna's maid rolled her eyes but obliged. Kya and Laverna left the room to take a quick shower and Kya put on one of the nighties furnished for guest in the guesthouse. Laverna was already lying down when Kya returned, she looked at Kya, raised the comforter in an inviting way. The next morning Kya woke up naked with cold large double "D" melons in her back. Neither said a word as they gather up their things, nor the ride to the airport.

Kya took the trip on the plane back to Little Pebbles alone, she took that hour to reflect on how much fun she had that weekend. Two trips in two different private plane to two different states, two different adventures but the same results was had, plenty of fun! She wouldn't make it home in time for church but enough time to listen to some music and relax with a drink because tomorrow would be her last night at the four-plex. These are the times when Kya missed Babette but she was glad she had a new home starting a better life. Kya paid the cab driver and lug herself inside she was dog tired so instead of listening to music she opted to take a bath and go to sleep.

Juane' picked Kya up Monday morning with a big grin on her face prompting Kya to ask her what's up. "Oh nothing, Juane' said it just that I got my friend Stanley over a Diamond Buick to set up a deal for you, here is his number call him as soon as you can he is expecting it." Kya took the card with the info on it and reminded Juane' that she would have to call during her lunch because Nykole doesn't like them to use work time for personal call. As soon as Kya clocked out for lunch she called Stanley over at Diamond Buick.

After a few minutes of being paged Stanley came to the phone, once Kya told him who she was he said he would be glad to sell her car and that in fact he has a few choices with her name on it. Before hanging up they made arrangements to meet that evening after work, then she called Willie so he would open the door and kind of watch over things as the furniture people load the furniture into the townhouse.

Since Juane' had a PTA meeting that evening so she wasn't able to bring Kya to the dealership leaving Kya to hopped on her friend the bus! She was thinking how nice Nykole was at work today, gave her important transaction to do and even told her goodnight have a good evening when she left for the day. Oh well no need to linger on that it's time to look at my new car. The bus put Kya off a block away from the Diamond Buick which made her curse herself for wearing six inch heels to work, the dealership was just closing but Kya could see a tall lanky guy with glasses sitting behind the desk so she knock on the glass door. The gentleman open and said are you Kya, welcome I have been waiting for you.

She test drove a Buick Enclave, and a dark blue Park Avenue which she fell in love with. Once back at the dealership Kya filled out paperwork and Stanley gave her a down payment figure. Now we did have a prospective buyer on the Park Avenue today who said they would be back on Thursday evening but if you can put down about nine or ten thousand today with a three hundred monthly payment for five years the car is yours. Kya did a quick calculation in her head she was short about three hundred and fifty dollars to even meet the nine thousand mark, but she told Stanley ok but she couldn't get it until tomorrow. Stanley agreed to hold the car for her at least until Wednesday, they shook hands and Kya left to catch the last bus back to the four-plex so she wouldn't have to walk or call a cab.

Now what to do, Kya kept asking herself. I could ask Juane' to loan me the money but money can break a friendship and for the first time in a while Kya felt she found a good friend in Juane'. Because she wanted to make sure the old lady knew how much she appreciate her kindness she gave Ms. Poer the earmarked money yesterday, so she dare not ask for it back and be an Indian giver. Then it hit her all of sudden, she would take the three hundred fifty from her till and put it back Friday morning before anyone noticed but how could she do it. Then she wondered to herself if she needed the car that bad enough to risk her job. Her answer was yes, so she devised a plan to sneak the money right after she counted her till for the evening, everyone else would be to busy doing the same to notice her putting it into an envelope and slide it in her purse.

Tuesday all day at work Kya was so nervous that she kept screwing up people deposit and even gave one customer too much money and another not enough. She recalled when she bought her plasma TV; she was short one hundred dollars so she took it from the till at work and replaced it two days later without a hitch so why was she so discombobulated this time? Well it's time to clock out and the deed had been done, now all Kya has to do it get out the door and over to the dealership, Juane' was waiting to give her a ride but just as Kya was walking out of the door Nykole said "Ms. Martinley I need to see you!" Kya heart was beating so loud that Grambling University could have much to its beat. After telling Juane' she would be a moment, Kya step in the wood shed to the rubber hose.

"Ms. Martinley, we seem to have a situation here. We are both adults and I'm sure you are aware of what situation I am referring to. The first time it happened I wasn't sure so I let it slide but I got you now read handed." Kya had to keep up the façade, she raised her eyebrows to give that I don't know or understand what you are talking about look? Nykole leaned forward placing her hand under her chin letting her elbow rest on the desk and gave Kya a stare that would have Leroy Jethro Gibbs proud. "Ok, Ms. Martinley Nykole said with a big grin, have it your way, I will see you tomorrow."

Glad to be out of that office Kya felt her spine was missing as she sloshed over to Juane' awaiting car. Even in unspoken words Kya knew Nykole somehow saw her, now she was wonder what was going to happen. She really didn't want to involve her friend; when Juane' asked what was wrong? Kya respond with a lie by telling her Nykole need her to sign some papers that need to be faxed first thing in the morning and she doesn't report work until ten. Juane' bought the lie because she turned her conversation to what kind of car Kya was going to buy. That put sort of a smile on Kya's face as she described the vehicle that might have cost her a job.

Kya took Juane' for a ride in her new car, they road up and down the avenue a couple of times before Kya drove Juane' back to the dealership to pick up her own car. As Kya drove away she was smiling for ear to ear because she had her new car. She appreciated her Jeep Liberty because it was given to her when she had no car but it wasn't in good condition when she got and baggers can't be choosey. Now she had to contact Willie to see if the furniture arrived ok because she was on her way to her new home.

Mystery Solved

Kya had to admit Willie and the movers set up the furniture nicely, so there wasn't much to move. So with Juane's help Kya was able to get her furniture set up just the way she wanted. It felt like heaven a nice roomy place, no noise, no trash and no Jackson and his dance team; well she had to admit she was going to miss Jackson's dance show. The only thing left was to create center pieces, decorations and what knots for the tables and walls. The next morning Kya was waiting for the shoe to drop with Nykole, nothing never happen she just continued to be nicer and nicer to her. Kya couldn't understand it but as long as she didn't make waves she figured Nykole was just blow smoke up her ass so she was safe.

It's Thursday morning and Kya hadn't gotten her usual medi-pedi on Wednesday because she wanted to get home and start on the décor of each room, her plan was to go right after work but just before the Merry Ladies meeting that night. Again as she and Juane' were leaving the evening Nykole ask to see Kya in her office. "I see you have a new car, it's nice and I also heard through the grapevine you moved into a new townhouse so things are going good for I presume? Nykole asked. "Well, my dear I got proof of your little thieving ass." Now take a look at this and she showed Kya a video tape of her counting her till letting a couple hundred dollar bill hit the floor picking them up and sliding the money in her lunch bag.

Kya just hung her head down; the jig was up there was the proof. Then she asked Nykole why hadn't she turned her in? Nykole uttered "Because my dear I have other plans for you and if you want to continue on the good life path that you are on, you will do exactly as I say from now on. I have two conditions first I want to switch clientele with you; I will trade McMillian and DJ Strongmath for Duvernay and McFarland." Kya shook her head no saying "I thought Merry Ladies were about making the clients happy and what if you are not what they want?" Nykole voiced loudly, "no problem that's when you convince them I am, secondly Nykole continued Barrows and I have a little side thing going and you will be a nice addition; this is between us three. You're to do whatever the client want, even sex now leave and close my door behind you."

Kya walked out of the office flabbergasted and speechless, it's a good thing Juane' was gone because she didn't want have to answer any questions plus Nykole specifically said things were between the three of them. Kya put herself in that predicament and Nykole being the evil person that she is will be taking full advantage of her stupid mistake. She drove home quiet, not even the smooth sounds of r&b music could pep her up tonight.

Kya pulled under her carport and just sat there, she even ignored Juane' call by picking up her cell phone of the passenger seat and dropping it into her purse. She just wasn't in the mood to talk or even try to hide what was going on. What she could use Kya thought was a good strong drink, backing her car out from under the carport she headed to Wally's early.

"Hello Kya, Susan said with a surprised expression, your early will you be sitting at the usual table?" Nodding her approval Kya followed Susan to the table and ordered a double scotch on the rocks which she basically gulped down and ordered another. Once the second drink arrived Kya gulped it down too and ordered a third along with an extra spicy order of chicken wings. Her mind was racing how can she get out of this, she wanted out of everything but again how?

By the time the other arrived Kya was hammered and waiting for her fourth drink. She jumped up and hugged Juane' rambling something about appreciating her friendship, patted Barbara and Dominicki on the shoulders saying they too were also good people.

Humph was the only thing she said when she turned to Nykole and Mr. Barrows, sat back down to finish her wings.

The Merry Ladies meeting went almost as usual, Kya was making rude comments and drinking heavily. Juane' was worried about her friend; she knew something was wrong because she never saw her behave like that. They even almost came to blows when Kya wanted another drink and Juane' intervened by telling the waiter not to bring it.

What made Kya realize she may have had too much to drink was when she slapped Juane' for asking her how many drinks she had already. After grabbing and hugging her Juane' whispered "whatever the problem is friend I'm here for you." Then like most drunks when they realize there wrong, Kya started to cry. Mr. Barrows adjourned the meeting and everyone left but not before Nykole sneeringly said to Juane' "some friend huh, guess you don't need any enemies?"

Before anybody knew it Kya ran outside tackled Nykole and the fight began. Barbara had made it to her car already but she saw the crowd gathering and circle back to Wally's front door. Once she saw Dominicki and Juane' pulling Kya and Nykole apart she slammed on the brakes and jumped out to help. Purses and their contents, weave pieces and shreds of clothing were everywhere, Nykole's halter top fall apart during the fight so Mr. Barrows offered her his jacket so she could cover up. "Bitch I'm not finish your dumb ass yet, you are going to pay and pay dearly! Kya make sure your ass is at work for seven!" Nykole shouted as she stomped away to her car and squealed away. Barbara, Juane' and Dominicki thank Susan for not calling the police like she started to and Kya apologize for actions and offered to pay for any damages that occurred; just let me know at next week's meeting.

By now Kya had sober up quite a bit but she went back into Wally's to get some black coffee before she drove home. Since she move to the townhouse the drive home from Wally's was only ten minutes away. Barbara, Mr. Barrows and Dominicki had said their goodnights again and left. Juane' stayed behind to make sure Kya was alright. "Girl, I don't know how your drunken ass managed to walk upright enough to tackle anybody but you did Juane' said laughing.

Now I don't know what's going on and like I said earlier I'm here to talk or do whatever I can do when you are ready." Kya thanked Juane' but she just didn't want to talk about it, she felt so stupid and embarrassed but as always she appreciated her concern and friendship, she just wanted to go home.

Friday morning found Kya lying in the bed feeling stiff, battered and bruised, she had to laugh at the silliness of her actions last night. Hell she didn't even know if she still had a job; speaking of job Kya figured she better get up and get ready. Barely moving Kya made it through showering, dressing and driving to work.

She was about ten minutes late arriving to the bank and of course Nykole was there unusually early and in the bank, the other unusual thing was that the candy red Escape was parked with no one in it. Kya walked to the door and knocked, Nykole answered then announced to someone that the other pussy was here. "Pussy Kya questioned, bitch what the hell you're talking about, if you think I'm scared we can go another round now."

"Oooo pretty and feisty I like her Nykole," Kya heard a woman voice say. Ignoring the voice Kya ask Nykole what did she have her there so early for? "Like I said bitch I got big plans for you, it was just a matter of time before you fucked up and now I got your pretty big ass in a noose," Nykole conveyed. "Enough of the cat fighting ladies the voice declared, let's get to business before the other get here. Kya you will meet with the client Monday thru Wednesday after work so not to interfere with Merry Ladies. The meeting with the client is at a hotel where you keep him company for an hour.

Once you're done with your tryst you should text this number saying the withdrawal is done. Captain Lewis or I will then pick up the money from the client and drop it into at a slotted post office box. Early on Monday's I pick up the money, count it and drop it off to my husband for deposit before the bank opens," Mrs. Barrows said as she step out of the shadow and directly into Kya's astonish face.

Now Nykole see to it that Ms. Martinley keep her date. While exposing a gun from her purse Mrs. Barrows said "you know I get real mean when people mess with my money." Then Mrs. Barrow strutted out of the bank into the candy red Ford Escape leaving Kya standing with her mouth wide open. "Close your mouth, this is some serious shit with more money to be made then working with Merry Ladies," Nykole shouted. Here is your client for tonight his name is Marvin; meet him at the Hotel Tiltom on Wrise Boulevard at seven fifteen then meet you can go on your Merry Ladies journey. Don't forget when you leave tonight text Captain Lewis cell now as before get out of my face and my office.

Kya worked all day with a queasy stomach, Nykole told her tonight would be her only Friday night date because the usual girl cancelled due to the flu. Damn how did I get myself into the predicament she repeatedly asked herself during lunch time? As she paced back and forth, sitting then standing Kya wonder if she can do it. She did take money as little as it was and if she want to maintain her new life style along with her job; lowering her head Kya concluded that she will have to prostitute herself. Juane' watched her friend through the break-room jarred open door with a worried looked on her face. She wanted to ask her what's was wrong but decided not to in hopes that she will come to her soon for help. Fully opening the door Juane' said "Kya are you ok, I hear you mumbling back here." Startled Kya responded yes I'm fine just hashing something out in my head.

The Letters and Vagabond

⌐

S itting in her Park Avenue on the parking lot of Hotel Tiltom, Kya was bracing herself for the worse. The hotel wasn't the best or in the best of neighborhoods but then again it wasn't in the worst so things could possibly go ok as she yet again talked aloud to herself. Kya knocked on the door and a deep voice said come in. Hi! I'm Kya and you must be Marvin she said with a fake smile, making a mental note to put vaseline on her teeth so her lips won't get stuck next time. The voiced from the bathroom said for her to have a drink and relax on the bed he would be right out. The next thing Kya heard was all kinds of farts with liquid stool plopping into the water, the toilet flushed and the voice came out.

Oh, hell no Kya yelled as she surveyed the guy in front of her. It was a customer that visited the bank frequently and he was known as Messy Marvin. "You have got to be kidding me; this has to be a joke or a test or something. Where is Nykole? Nykole come on out you can't hate me that much please let this be a joke!" Kya cried out as she searched the room. "Hey you need to calm your ass down; I paid very good money for just an hour with you. Now I may not look like much but I got money, lots of money but no one to love. Beside Marvin continued to say love is over rated, I buy my pussy we may or may not dine then I'm on to live my life the way I want to, dirt and all."

Marvin pulled back the covers motioning Kya to join him. Kya walked slowly over while loosening up her leopard print Gucci wrap dress. She was lying stiffly across the bed as Marvin started too leered

110

over her, stopped and began to suck on her toes. First the little toe, then the next until he reach the big toe where he really went to work with smacking sounds and slob running down his face. Silent tears started flowing and Kya started praying. As he rose to touch her leg, Kya began to tremble from the disgust of this stinky man touching her. He smelled of sour ass, garbage, shit, spit, under arm mustiness and athlete feet; in short he smelled like all be damned. "Hell" Kya yelled "get off me you crusty old fool" as she sprang from the bed into the bathroom to vomit.

Kya returned from the bathroom finding Marvin sitting at the table naked sporting a hurt look on his face. As she headed to the door to leave Marvin exclaimed "Oh Ms. Prissy we still a little business to take care of, I don't care if you have to hold your nose and cover your face with a paper bag that pussy is mines for thirty more minutes. He leaped forward to grab Kya who manage do dodge his reach. He landed on the floor did a tuck and roll and got up running, all Kya could see was gray bobbing balls one step ahead of his feet coming toward her. "Please Marvin I can't do this, the punishment is not worth the crime, is there some kind of compromise we can come to?" begged Kya. Nah! Was the only thing Kya heard as she was thrown to the floor and mulled like an animal!

Wait! Wait! Can't you at least take off your sock? They are off Marvin replied through liquored kisses on her neck. Kya could not let this happen; she felt another round of vomit sitting in her throat. Marvin continued his assault on her body, rough whiskers tearing at her soft skin as he kiss down her breast onto her stomach. This can't be happening Kya keep yelling, I would let it and before Kya knew it she reached out grab the bourbon bottle sitting on the floor next to the bed and crack the old fool over the head. The blow made Marvin body go limp instantly leaving him to collapse on top of Kya. Blood started oozing from the back of his head down his neck and dripped on to Kya. Oh my goodness Kya screamed again Marvin! Marvin; he didn't answer.

Kya rolled the bleeding smelly man off of her and onto the floor; her head was pounding as she tried to figure out what the hell to do next. I know, Kya thought I will get the hell out of here. She then fixed her clothes, straighten her hair, grab her purse, peeked out of the door and did sprints to her car driving away and not looking back. Reaching her townhouse Kya open the door and just plopped down on her new leather sectional and cried. What was she going to do, being a call girl was bad enough but prostituting to degenerates was not good at all.

Kya knew she shouldn't have taken the three hundred and fifty dollar from her till at work, but she had to get that car beside she took five hundred before to pay for her plasma and put it back. She loved that car and didn't want the other prospective buyer to get it. Now she is a hell of a pickle. "Marvin" Kya whispered I do hope he is ok, maybe I should call an ambulance or at least the hotel front desk to go check on him."

Just as Kya decided to just ride back out to the Hotel Tiltom, Juane' arrived suddenly wanting to talk with her as a good friend. Kya asked Juane' if she mind if they took a ride while they talk. "Sure where would you like to ride to?" Juane' asked. "Nowhere in particular said Kya I just wanted to cruise in my new car." As Kya drove Juane' began to voice her concern for her, she also let Kya know once again that she was there for her. "Good" Kya said as she turned the corner on to the street of the hotel where police, ambulance and news reporters hovered, "then I'm going to need your help to get out of this as she pointed to the commotion" and then sped away fast. Driving just above the speed limit Kya explained what happened and how she got into the mess in the first place.

Still in Kya's car parked under the carport the stunted Juane' responded "are you serious Kya? You have definitely gotten yourself in a mess. Why didn't you come to me, I could have loaned your ass the three fifty or you could've found another car. Damn! I bet Nykole is loving every minute of it." You know she is recoiled Kya, listen I just couldn't ruin our friendship by borrowing from you and I have come to love this new lifestyle. Had I gotten fired I wouldn't be able to afford this townhouse. Without Merry Ladies and the money I make I couldn't have bought a house full of nice expensive furniture, you know that I spent almost every penny at the furniture store. I was short and Stanley said he would only hold the car for a day, how was I to know Nykole had a camera specially trained on me.

"Juane please don't say anything, I appreciate your offer of help but now I am in too deep, that creep Marvin, if he is not dead, will probably press charges against me if Mrs. Barrows doesn't kill me first. I'm scared to even show up for work Monday because I had to cancel my Merry Ladies date with Jacob tonight, don't think I will make my date with Laverna tomorrow."

After talking a couple more hours, Juane' convinced Kya to continue her routine that weekend and on Monday come to work pretending nothing happened. As she was leaving Juane' told Kya she would pray for her and to watch herself. Her last words before driving away were she was going to find out how Marvin was doing, go take a long hot bath, use bubbles, and clear your mind. I will call you later.

Kya had a feeling things were going to come to a halt with the bank job and Merry Ladies and it was all her fault; why did she have to be so impatience? Juane' was right she could've let the other person buy the Park Avenue, but it was sweet car; fully loaded the colored she wanted and the price wasn't bad either. Now all Kya wanted to do was rest, she took Juane' suggestion and then slept until three the next day waking only once to talk to Juane' when she called to check on her and to inform her Marvin was alive and in the hospital.

The screaming alarm clock woke her; Kya reached over and hit the snooze button repeating that action a couple of times before she actually got up. Rummaging through her closet to find a pair of shoes to go with one of the dresses she bought in Ballas, Texas Kya came across the dress she wore the second time her and Bruce had sex, it was in the restaurant bathroom. That made her smile as she thought about the good time she had with him and much like now she is dating a married man and a woman, geeze where and when did she sell her soul for money was the important questions Kya asked herself. Oh well no time to dwell on it was Kya's thoughts I've got to get ready for my date and when you're out with Laverna you have to look your best; Laverna will settle for nothing less.

· Laverna beat Kya to the restaurant and was already eating their favorite appetizers of potato skins that were fully loaded with cheese, bacon, sour cream, jalapeno peppers and chives. She motion for Kya to come on over and join her. "Well I see someone is hungry." Kya said as she sat down at the table. "I couldn't wait for you, this is the first time I had to eat all day," Laverna replied with a mouth full the scrumptious taters.

Laverna continued on to say that she was opening a new restaurant in Little Pebble but before she could come there was a problem at one of her Alabama store so she had to travel to Birmingham before she could go home and be the fabulous person before her. As she talked she noticed Kya staring at something or someone behind her, so she glanced back to see. "Oh I'm sorry, said Kya I thought I saw somebody I knew, so what were you saying?'

"Dear you need a good stiff one" Laverna said as she motion for the waiter to come over, when he arrived Laverna order to good strong long island ice tea. After two more tall glasses of the fermented tea the ladies were giggling and giddy, Kya was relaxed and feeling good. Laverna slid closer to her in the booth, the two sat there talking into each other's face having a good time as if they were the only two in Magine Fine Cusine Restaurant.

Kya wasn't sure when Laverna placed her hand on her knee, but she knew instantly when a probing finger entered her womanhood. She looked at Laverna and Laverna replied "Shhh! just let it happen no one can see under the table and we are sitting in a booth. Relax let me take some of that stress off your shoulders, Kya's thighs went limp to the sweet strokes of Laverna's well-manicured finger.

The waitress comes over to see if they needed anything else, shocking Kya back to where they were. Laverna replied with a stern no but Kya just sat there surprisingly not embarrass but perturbed for the intrusion. Laverna gave the young lady a hundred dollars to leave them alone for a while, she refused saying the restaurant will be closing in ten minutes, that's all she will allow and she walked away mumbling.

"Well" Kya said "I need to excuse myself, be right back." She headed toward the ladies room but stopped dead in her tracks when she saw Marvin sitting outside the restaurant window that she had to pass to get to her destination. He was sitting there laughing and mouthing something to her. Kya blinked her eyes to make sure that he was what she was really seeing. When she looked again he was gone. So she continued on to the restroom.

Upon returning to the table Laverna was ready to leave. She asked Kya to accompany her to a night club, but Kya decline because either she had too much to drink, very tired or going crazy. Whatever the case maybe she was going home, she had some things to work out in her head and she wouldn't be good company. The two parted ways with a kiss, Laverna got in her limo and Kya in her Park Avenue which Laverna loved once she saw it. On the drive home Kya knew she had to take care of unfinished business so tonight was the night, it wouldn't undo the damage that was done but it would free her mind mending the hole in her heart.

At the townhouse Kya hadn't discovered her favorite room like in the four-plex so the dining table would have to do. She went to her desk to retrieve the letters from Bruce, she read all three of them with teary eyes, wrote a response then took the check from Bruce's lawyer and signed it over to Lois to use for little Kenya however she saw fit. Next she wrote a three letters to her friends back home in Ponde, Louisiana and one to Juane'.

The first letter was to Airis. Kya told her how she was proud she has gotten her life together and found a good man that will be everything she needed. Also she mention a little of how and why thing happen to be with her and Bruce, she didn't do it to be deceitful. Their first encounter happened when she was drunk and lonely and he was trouble and lonely too. She hopes that she would forgive her and to have a wonderful happy life.

The second letter was to Bailey. She started with Bailey and Tanja sitting in the tree K-I-S-S-I-N-G. Hello my friend, I not sure if you figured out that I actually set you up with Tanja. I knew her from one of my anatomy classes at Ponde U, she too was just as confuse as you were about her sexuality. She saw me talking to you one day when we were having lunch in the mall and mention that she saw you pondering several times at the Four Leaf. On the night you meet if you would have looked closer you would have seen me sitting in my car after driving Tanja there. With that said you can put two and two together. I do love you and hope that you have found forgiveness in your heart toward me.

She had to think long and hard about the last letter. It was the reason why she ran from Ponde.

> My dearest and best friend Chandenise, I have tried to write this letter so many times but it's been hard for me. I want you to understand what happen then maybe in time you will forgive me so I'm unburdening on paper knowing it will never reach you. Although I wish you were here to hear my side of the story. It was a drunken accident that started us but lust that kept it going and I have been beating myself up every day since; well I guess I didn't beat myself up enough because I continued on with the affair anyway.

> I want you to know that Bruce is the best man that I've ever had to come into my life; I see why you changed your wild ways to settle down with him. I'm writing this letter to clear my conscious and heart. I know you will never get to read this because you have gone home to meet your maker which is partially my fault but the other is yours because you forgot you were supposed to be in love with him. Love him not his fame, power and money. You belittled him taking his manhood and I gave it back. You also forgot the little things are what matter and to listen to him being his best friend in life. You know as well as I know now that Bruce is the most tender, passionate lover there is to be with. He is kind, gentle and generous. When you are in his presence you forget your troubles, worries and that anything or anybody else exist.

Every time he laid me down on the bed I kept thinking Kya you shouldn't be doing this, but once he placed his warm hands on my body it left an imprinted trail of heat that boiled down to my soul. Every time we kiss I was blinded to the fact that he was yours and oh my goodness when he licks my womanly parts, mmm! Bruce's tongue would start with my breast down along my stomach to linger on my clit. Then that oh wonderful tongue would enter my sweet hole with the security of a tampon, work its way around to my sphincter letting me have an orgasm that rates a twelve on the Richter scale. Next he would enter my honey cave with his very impressive man meat delivering a tune of slow methodical rhythm and unselfish patience causing me to squirt out an abundance of love juice. Just as I'm nearing the end of my sexual blissful convolution Bruce would hits his sexual spurt; we shutter together. Afterwards we lie in each other arms soaking wet, tired and sharing a cigarette; unbelievably happy.

I couldn't give him up! The above paragraph describes it all. He became the drug I look forward to taking so I could feel the euphoria of love.

Rest in peace my friend and despite what happen you were truly my best friend and I did and do still love you.

Kya then address all five envelopes to the perspective person, put a stamp on them and placed them in her purse to be mailed in the morning. She really did feel at ease after unloading her inner most troubles on paper. Kya decided all that sadness needed to be remedy by happiness so she called Jacob McFarland. It was late but after missing their date last night he had called her over twenty times. He answered the phone on the first ring and was so happy that Kya called that he agreed to meet her at her home. After giving him directions, Kya hung up, ran upstairs to take a shower and put on her sexiest lounging dress.

McFarland showed up forty-five minutes later carrying a slab of ribs from Whole Hog Café, a bottle of wine and a new cd. Because Kya new furniture was white they moved to the small patio out back. McFarland only stayed long enough to eat and assure himself that Kya was alright. He told her that he was looking forward to next Friday because he wanted to take her to Vegas for the whole weekend so she should clear her calendar. As he kissed her goodnight he complimented her on her beauty and home then left singing a tune.

Kya gathered all the containers and bones to put in the dumpster that was located about five feet outside her gate. Heading back toward the yard Kya caught a glimpse of someone peeking in between her townhouse and her neighbors. It was Marvin; he was just sitting there mouthing something yet again so she ran inside to grab her phone, flashlight and taser gun. She went back outside to check but no one was there. Kya figured maybe she was really tired after all it was two fifty in the morning, so she was going to bed and fast.

Duped the Party's Over

K ya thought she was going crazy but when she saw Marvin
hanging outside the church, the grocery store and the bakery
on that Sunday she knew something was up. Monday would be the
day she would find out because today she had planned on staying
inside and doing nothing. She called Juane' to tell her what was
going on and she agreed Kya should stay put and wait for her to
arrive to keep her company. Every so often she would look outside
her window to see if Marvin was there but he wasn't, by the time
Juane' came she was a nervous wreck.

With her friend there Kya felt at ease. They talk and talk and
talk, every time Juane' even thought about leaving Kya would start
another conversation of gossip; Juane's favorite kind. So desperate
for Juane' company Kya even told her the tale of Chandenise
and Bruce; substituting her name with Sharon and omitted her
involvement altogether. Juane' listened to a few more stories but
it was Sunday night and unlike Kya she had to make sure her kids
were getting prepared for bed. She said her goodbyes and left.

Tired from broken sleep yet dressing for work Kya wondered
what the day had in stored for her. She drove to the post office to
drop off her letters and then headed to work, upon arriving she
noticed the candy red Ford Escape meaning Mrs. Barrows was inside
probably with Nykole plotting on her punishment. Kya didn't want
any part of that so she drove past the bank to the local Wendy's,
ordered breakfast and sat a table where she had an obscured view of
the bank. The one view that was clear was Marvin; he was walking

on the opposite side of the street from Wendy's heading toward the bank.

Kya decided to wait until her co-workers arrived and the occupants at the bank now leave before she goes in, knowing that meant she would be late. By the time she finished eating and on her second cup of coffee, Kya saw the Ford Escape make a left turn at the traffic light heading toward the interstate. She called the bank and hung as soon as Dominicki answered the phone so she knew the coast was possibly clear. Kya discarded her trash and arrived at the same time as Juane' was pulling into her assigned parking spot.

Juane' walked over to Kya saying don't panic but I see Marvin, hopefully he is just here as a customer. Marvin was standing in a short line of customers waiting for the doors to open in five minutes. They had to pass right by him to get inside the bank. Kya could smell him the closer she got and once she past him he reached out and slapped her on the ass with a huge smile, revealing the mustard colored teeth that once tried to kiss her. Squealing in disgust she almost knocked down Captain Lewis as he opened the door for her and Juane'.

Business as usual was Nykole attitude toward Kya, which was shocking to Juane' and Kya. "It's the calm before the storm Juane' said to Kya. I wonder why Mr. Barrows hasn't been in yet." Kya said "I don't know but I still see Marvin hanging around at the tobacco store across the street." The pair watched Messy Marvin through the drive-thru window as he dug in the cigarette container outside the store.

Kya was glad it was quitting time but she lost track of where Marvin was in between waiting on customers and balancing her till for the night. Nykole left around five once the lobby closed and Mr. Barrows had neither showed nor called which had Kya even more nervous; it wasn't like him. With the bank shut up like Fort Knox Captain Lewis walked the ladies to their cars, as Kya was pulling away he stopped her and said tonight better go off without a hitch or your ass is grass.

Kya didn't ask him what he meant because she already knew. It was six thirty and she had to meet with another client at eight according to the note Nykole slipped to her before she left. No name just Hotel Tiltom, room number three nineteen and a time. Kya raced home to change, she had made up her mind if she was going to do this she wasn't going to be glamorous at all, just plain Jane for an hour. She poured herself a tall glass of Crown Royal put on a pair of worn jeans, tank top and tennis shoes. Kya read her mail, downed the rest of the drink and left.

She was really buzzing but that was the only way she was going to get through the ordeal with whoever was her john for the night. Damn a john Kya thought I'm a prostitute no matter how you look at, I sleep with people for money even though it's against my will. She parked the Park Avenue at the back of the hotel, found the room but before going in she took a big swig of whiskey from the flask in her purse and knocked.

The person told Kya to come on in. she opened the door to find a naked man standing with his back to her pouring a drink. He turned around fully erected. He told Kya no time to waste with introductions let's get this over with, my wife is having a baby at any minute and I have to be there to see my son born. Kya stripped down to her birthday suit, hell he didn't even wait for her to get in the bed. He took her right there bent over a chair, five minutes later it was over he was getting dressed and off he went.

No name or anything but at least he didn't stink and appeared to have some kind of hygiene Kya was thinking and she took a whore bath in the sink. She still was wondering how long she would have to do it, my goodness it was only three hundred and fifty dollars. She could only imagine what would happen if it was more but knowing Nykole it could've been a penny she just wanted to humiliate Kya and doing a pretty good job at. Dressed and texting the code words to Captain Lewis as she walked down the stairs of the hotel to her car Kya spotted Marvin sitting on the hood of the Park Avenue.

"Oh I'm not good enough for you huh?" Marvin said to Kya as she tried to side step him and into her car. "Look bitch my money is good and you owe me an hour worth of snatch and I don't care if we have to do it in the back seat of this nice car." Kya was scared but she continued on to her car. Marvin wasn't having it he slammed her head against the car trying to rip off her jeans. Kya screamed for help! That didn't stop Marvin he just kept going. When he took out his penis Kya could have sworn she saw green fog came out with it.

Sick to her stomach, she struggled and continued to yell for help but no one came. Just when she thought she would have to be raped by a crusty man she remembered a self-defense move from the movie "Miss Congeniality". Once she implemented the "SING" move Marvin fell to the ground giving her time to get inside her car. He then got up grabbed ahold of the door with both hands just as Kya started the engine. He wouldn't let go of the handle even as Kya drugged him around the parking lot. "Get off my car man" Kya kept yelling but Marvin wouldn't budge. Kya slammed on brakes sending him rolling and as luck would have it he ended up by the only entrance/exit of the hotel parking lot.

They were at a standstill, Marvin blocking the exit with his pants around his ankles and Kya in her car. So she did the only thing she could do, she gunned the car in hopes that the smelly bastard would move but he didn't. Kya hit him with the car and kept going. She could hear him hollering as she drove off, it hurt her to hurt another human being but after all he was trying to violate her body. Looking in the rear view mirror Kya saw some people gathering around to help Marvin. "Oh great Kya said out loud to herself, now somebody shows up!"

Kya made it home, practically jumping out of the car before she could get it stopped. She was shaking so bad she couldn't get the door to her townhouse open. Now she has finally done it, from almost illegal to illegal to attempted murder to murder; a new low in her life. Nothing left to do but wait for the police to show up. She had to relax or as relax as she could get for a person in her situation. The thought of killing herself entered him mind for a brief second but she knew that was a sin so that idea was nixed.

She had no one to call, her partner Chandenise was dead. Bailey and Airis weren't talking to her anymore and Bruce was in jail. Kya could've called Juane' but she didn't want her to be involved any more than she already was, she has kids to think about so Kya once again didn't answer her cell when Juane' called. She even thought about calling Jacob or Laverna for help but they too have families and probably don't want them to know they have been consorting with a paid escort. "I know Kya exclaimed music, it always calms the savage beast."

Kya put in all six of the cds Jacobs made especially for her, grab a bottle of whiskey and on to the awaiting bubble bath. She was tired of thinking and fighting about things, she will have to take her lumps as they come. While she soaked in the tub she Juane' knocking at the door screaming for her to answer the door. She was saying something about something being on the news. "I'm not going away Kya so open the damn door!" Juane' yelled.

Before she woke up the neighbors Kya grabbed her robe off the bathroom hook putting it on as she headed downstairs to open the door. It's about time you opened the door woman turn on the news!" Juane' loudly voice. I got a feeling you and I both will need this drink Kya said as she poured two glasses of whiskey and turned on the TV. There on the sixty four inch screen was Marvin's face. It was a story about the hit and run being the second attempt on his life. He was taken to the hospital but was pronounced dead upon arrival.

The victim was identified as Marvin Georges; a once prominent business man until he lost his wife and three daughters in a drunk driving accident ten years ago where the car he was driving collided head on with his wife's car as he turned the corner at a high speed. Before Mr. George expired he told the police a tale of a prostitution ring being ran within a local bank naming Nykole Washington, assistant branch manager as the alleged ring leader.

When authorities went to the home of Ms. Washington for questioning; they found Mr. Barrows the branch manager sitting in his car dead from an apparent gunshot wound. Mrs. Barrows his wife and Ms. Washington have yet to be reached for comment at the moment, authorities has also issued a BOLO and investigation is ensuing. "Wow!" they both said in unison. Juane' spoke first saying it's all over, the money, gifts and the job. "To hell with that Juane' Kya blurted out Mr. Barrows is dead and I killed Marvin, yeah he didn't die instantly but the injuries he sustained from the car's blow still killed him."

"Kya you know that we are going to go to jail and I may lose my kids, where the hell is Nykole?" Juane' said through tears. "I know my dear friend was Kya response, let me see if Barbara or Dominicki has heard anything," as she pick the phone to make that call. Dominicki didn't answer the phone but Barbara said she was packing to get out of town before the police arrived and Dominicki may have done so already.

Juane' decided she wanted to leave and have a talk with her kids; she didn't want them to hear it on the news or from anybody else. "Be strong my friend and I will be too, I'm sure the cops will want to talk with us both so I'm going to turn myself in and I suggest you do the same after you talk with your kids," voiced Kya as she hugged Juane' goodbye. Kya sat there watching the new all evening, Nykole was caught trying to get on a plane to Canada but Mrs. Barrows was still nowhere to be found the reporter announced.

Tuesday morning Kya arrived at the police station bright and early, she wanted to get things over with as soon as possible. When she announced who she was to the desk sergeant she got a surprise reaction. All of a sudden the sergeant and two other cops drew their weapon on her. They shouted for her to place her hands behind her back, as she complied one officer grabbed her purse and begin to search it.

From there everything went so fast that Kya's head was spinning. It's seems when Nykole was apprehended she named Kya and the Barrowses as the ring leaders of both Merry Ladies the escort service and of the prostitution ring. She had documents with Kya signatures on them which listed the client's name, times, dates and monetary amount. During the interrogation Kya was presented with several documents to verify that it was her handwriting. Some were and some were that of Mr. Barrows.

Kya was kicking herself for signing documents without first reading all of them, she knew better than that. She told the officers that she thought she was signing off on bank reconciliations and or bank related stuff. Nykole had to have slipped those papers underneath or with bank documents so that her signature seeped through. She maintained her innocents citing that those illegal services were going on long before she arrived in Little Pebbles and she wouldn't say another word without her attorney present.

Sitting in the courtroom Kya looked around to see a familiar faces. Bailey and Airis came to show their support, which Kya hoped that mean they forgave her of her infidelity. Once the judge took the bench the prosecutor stated his case, the last thing Kya remembered was a commercial.